# No Tragedy Like Mine

NO TRAGEDY LIKE MINE

ISBN: 978-1-7923-8107-2

Published by:  ASG Publishing

## CHAPTER 1

Reflecting on the pain and agony this man has put me through, I said to myself, his ass needs to die in this hospital! I continued to urgently walk through the corridor of a hospital in New Jersey on a bright Saturday afternoon. This was a weekend that I decided to let my hair rest. Wearing one of my comfortable outfits with my hair straightened and parted, I made a right turn and stopped at the nurse's desk to ask for directions to Daymon's room. The overworked nurse gathered her belongings before clocking out. Her shift was coming to an end. My seriousness was obvious, and my demeanor could not be ignored.

"I'm looking for Daymon Shepard's room, can you tell me where he is?"

"Are you his wife?"

"No, I'm a friend. My name is Kim Adams."

The phone rang and the nurse told me to wait until she was finished the phone call. Just then, two other nurses came to the front desk. The nurse put the caller on hold, gave some papers to the two nurses, and found the time to tell me about the visiting hours.

"Visiting hours end at 8pm.  He is in the last room down that hall."

Then, she pointed me in the direction of the room that Daymon was in.  I took my time walking to his room.  I saw the patients in the other rooms.  Some with loved ones and some were all alone looking lifeless as if they were on their death beds.

I stood in front of a closed door at the end of the hall.  I took a deep breath, turned the door handle and witnessed a lady old enough to be my mother spitting on Daymon's chest.

"You got what you deserved!"

The look on her face led me to believe that she had been crying and did not care if she was caught spitting on the patient in this god-forsaken hospital.

"Excuse me.  How do you know Daymon?"

She gave me another disturbing look that said, why are you asking me questions.

I said, "Despite what this may seem, Daymon is my sister's boyfriend."

"Oh really. Why are you here?" She replied.

"I wanted to see if he was still alive."

"He's still holding on, but he doesn't look good at all. Only God knows his fate now. By the way, Daymon was my nephew's lover. His name was Eugene. I just found out about them a few days ago. So, did you know Eugene is dead?"

"No. I didn't know him."

"Sit down child. Tell me about your sister."

"By the way, I'm Mabel and you are?"

"I'm Kim."

Mabel took her seat first. I sat in the chair near Daymon's bed and took a deep breath. The beeping devices connected to Daymon chimed in harmony as we sat there in the hospital room. I looked in Mabel's eyes from across the room and felt no fear.

In my mind, I wondered...how much detail should I give this woman?

"We are four years apart. Me being the oldest, I had to look after her a lot.

We stood up for each other and I would take the blame for her mistakes sometimes. My dad was a manager for the phone company and my mother was a RN that worked at a demanding hospital in DC."

"I see you're going to give me your life story."

"You asked, so I'll briefly tell you about our childhood then bring up to the present."

Mabel smirked, "Honey, I got time. My niece has a flat tire. She's waiting for the roadside service to help her. We had Gene's, well Eugene's home going service yesterday and I stayed with family members. One of the cousins told us her version of the story and we came to see this boy. It was heavy on my mind to get down here to see if he was able to talk and tell us what happened. So, we're on our way back down to Petersburg, VA today or tomorrow. Believe you me...I got time! My niece knows nothing about changing a tire. Honey, the poor girl tried to get her cousin to come back and help her. She didn't have any tools to take the tire off the car. Besides all that, honey, my nephew had a secret lifestyle, and I didn't know a lot of his friends. I knew he spent a lot of time with Daymon. So, paint the picture honey. Tell me what you know."

There was a brief moment of silence in the room.  Mabel gave me her full attention.

"My sister Morgan was always the popular one that loved to wear the latest fashion. Unfortunately, she was always in the wrong place at the wrong time.  She was a very attractive light skin female that was caught up in the video model world when she was in her early twenties.  That didn't turn out well for her as a young adult in school."

"She modeled for magazines.  She posed nude a few times, but she had too much class to be nude at every photo shoot."

"When our father died, she broke down and couldn't fully rebound after his death.  He was the one that got her into modeling. He always encouraged us to follow our dreams and plan for the future."

"What happen to your father?" Inquired Mabel.

"Cancer."

"Jesus, they should've come up with a cure for that by now!" exclaimed Mabel.  "I have seen too many people die from that damn disease."

"I agree!"

I looked out the window and sighed. All this talk about my dad and my sister was making me depressed. I stood up and walked to Daymon's bed and stared at his short light skin body for a few seconds.

I looked in Mabel's direction. "My father met Daymon and seemed to like the guy. However, he told Morgan not to fall in love too quick. He urged her to find out about his past and his future. Shortly after my father's death Morgan started drinking all the time. She stopped modeling and was taking acting classes. Then she got involved in photography. She was really into photography. I spent time with her before the holidays and she showed me the awesome pictures she was selling."

Mabel interjected. "Tell me how they met! That's what you haven't mentioned."

"I was just about to tell you!"

"Daymon worked at a department store as a project manager for the photography and creative design team. Morgan was working with professional photographers that were doing a photo shoot for the store. Daymon and Morgan were introduced to each other when she displayed her shots on the computer screen during the photo shoot. She told me that he convinced her to try on some of the new garments that were going to be on the internet and in the magazines. She said that he told her not only was she a good photographer, but she was also good looking too! Naturally, Morgan fell back into her model mode. While dealing with Daymon, she got involved with purchasing the clothes for the department store. Ever since then, Daymon and Morgan were hanging tight. I went out with them from time to time. You know...restaurants, clubs, shopping...you understand. They fell in love. Three years have gone by and here we are in this hospital."

"But what happened? What do you know about my nephew's death?"

"My sister called me in the afternoon one day when I was at a cookout with some friends. I was in the middle of tasting the best seafood salad that I've ever had in my life when she called me on my cell phone. She was in a good mood. She had gotten her hair done that day and she was anxious to see if Daymon liked the new style."

I pulled out my cell phone to show the picture that Morgan sent to me showing off her new long hair style.

"That was the last time I heard from her, and no one knows where she is."

Mabel was looking at me intensely. "You mean she's missing? Jesus! I lost my sisters, but not like that honey. One died from natural causes and the other died from Cancer. I understand some of your pain."

With her palm facing up, Mabel offered her hand to hold. I extended my arm and held her hand. All of a sudden, Mabel gently squeezed my hand and started praying.

"God give Kim the ability to make it through these tough times and help us find out how all this happened. In Jesus name. Amen."

Mabel looked at Kim and said, "I know there's more to this story child."

"Yes, I'm not done."

Using my free hand, I wiped the tears from my eyes.

"Let's continue," Mabel said.

My mind started to wander. I had to regain my composure before I spoke.

"Morgan took some time off and drove up to Daymon's house from Maryland a day early to spend some time with him. She planned to surprise Daymon in New Jersey with her new hairdo and discuss moving in with him.

Morgan called to tell me that she was on the highway heading north to stay at Daymon's new house. She said that she would call when she got there. Her battery was low, and she forgot her charger. So, she kept the conversation short. So, like I said, that was the last time I talked to her."

## CHAPTER 2

## KIM

I paused and looked at the hospital floor for a while.

"Are you okay?  If you have to cry, let it all out.  I've done my share of crying child...believe me."

"Yes, I'm okay.  I'm just trying to remember everything that happened thus far."

Mabel wiggled around to find some comfort in the dated hospital chair that was in the room.  I frowned as I stared at Daymon's unconscious body in the bed with all the hospital instruments connected to him. Mabel's gaze drew my attention.  My eyes drifted in her direction.  She was politely waiting for me to tell her more.

"I live in Maryland, about four hours away. I've never been to Daymon's new house, I just know that Daymon moved from White Plains, NY to Hoboken, NJ.  Right outside of NY.  I thought about calling the police, but the Maryland Police Department would not be able to help me without an address and a description of the issue."

I started to concentrate harder. "Hold on, let me think. After getting the call from Morgan, I woke up and sat on the side of the bed the next morning. I looked around the room for my phone."

I sat down and really concentrated on the events that took place. "I saw my phone on the floor next to the surge protector. I picked up the phone and disconnected it from the charger. I checked my call log, voicemail, and email. There wasn't a text nor phone call from Morgan. I looked at the ceiling and began to cry because I believed something bad was going on and I wasn't there to help my sister. I went downstairs in my townhouse to make some coffee. I paced back and forth in the kitchen until I remembered that I wrote her new work phone number on the calendar in the kitchen. I called, but it was a Sunday, and the office was closed. However, I was determined to find my sister no matter what."

I got up and started to pace back and forth in the hospital room. I was rubbing my hands together as if I was trying to wipe the sweat from my palms.

Taking deep breaths to cope with the racing emotions of being uncertain about the outcome of my dilemma. I was worried and nervous like a criminal in a courtroom awaiting the verdict from the jury. Despite my efforts, I wondered if I had done enough to find my sister.

Mabel was persuading me to talk about everything I knew about her nephew and her nephew's lover. Unfortunately, I didn't know her nephew and I gave her the 411 about my sister and Daymon. I looked around the room trying to think of things to say.

"Sweetie, I can tell you're scared. Let's see if this hospital has some decent coffee. Do you want some coffee?"

I sighed, "Yes."

"Let's find some. There has to be a cafeteria somewhere in this place."

At that point, Mabel took her time getting out of the outdated hospital chair. Once she got up, she stood in one position, fixed her clothes, and grabbed her purse.

I said, "Are you ready?"

"Sure am! Let's get moving. We need to get away from this poor soul here anyway. Lord knows what's going to happen to...what's this boy's name again?" Mabel paused and frowned with confusion.

"Daymon."

"Yes, that's it. Only the LORD knows the fate of his poor soul."

We took our time walking out of the room. An RN came into the room to check Daymon's vital signs.

I said, "Excuse me," with a low subtle voice. "Where is the cafeteria? We need some coffee."

"It's on the first floor. Just read the signs on the wall when you get down there. It's about a ten-minute walk from here."

"Thanks!"

"I can use some myself," said the RN.

Mabel smiled at the RN and replied, "I know what you mean."

Mabel and I started walking toward the elevator.

"So, did you ever get the police involved Kim?"

Mabel pressed the down button to call for the elevator. Ding! The elevator doors opened. I let Mabel walk into the elevator first. She pressed the button for the first floor.

"Yes, my dad's friend Frank is a detective. Frank is working with the lead detective that is assigned to the case. His name is Richard Johnson. They didn't find any clues, nor did they find any leads. They questioned Daymon thoroughly, but he cooperated with the police, and they did not have any evidence to arrest him at that time. It's like my sister disappeared without a trace. Just like the kids on the milk carton."

The elevator slowed down. Ding! The elevator doors opened to a narrow hallway with an aroma of delightful food. The smell of bacon led us in the right direction as we saw people coming and going with cartons of food.

Silver tables could be seen throughout the first floor while we made our way through the cafeteria. I spotted the metal coffee

containers and lead Mabel toward them. I
turned slightly to her right and pointed at a
small silver square table with four chairs.

"That's a good table over there."

We maneuvered through the rows of tables and
chairs. The chatter from the doctors and
family members of the patients was a bit
loud. When we got to the table, Mabel put
her purse on it. She stuck her hand inside
the purse to grab her purple wallet.

Mabel handed me a ten-dollar bill and said,
"I like my coffee with three containers of
cream and six packets of sugar."

"Okay. I'll get it for you."

I went over to the slightly messy counter
where the coffee containers were. Mabel
felt something hard inside her purse as she
placed her wallet back in it. She didn't
remember putting much in her purse besides
the bare essentials. But low and behold,
there was another cell phone in her purse.
I looked back to see what she was doing.

I realized Mabel was looking at me from afar
with a confused look on her face, wondering
if I put the cell phone in her purse. She

knew it couldn't have been me because I was in her eyesight the entire time.

Mabel still had that perplexed look on her face as I walked back to the table with the coffee.

I took my seat and asked, "What's wrong?"

I slid the coffee to her along with her change. Mabel pressed the power button on the cell phone and slid the phone to me.

Mabel said, "Well, I'm trying to figure something out. I'm at a loss for words."

"Why are you showing me your phone?" I frowned and asked.

Mabel reached into her purse and pulled out her flip phone and said, "This is my phone. I don't know whose phone that is child. I don't know how that got in my purse."

I picked up the phone and started pressing buttons. The phone was locked, and the battery was low.

I pressed a few numbers, but the phone didn't unlock. At that time, Mabel was stirring her coffee trying to figure out whose phone that was. Naturally, she called her husband to ask him if he knew anything about the phone.

"Let me call my husband Robert. He might know about this phone."

I put the phone down and finished adding cream and sugar to my cup of coffee. I was stirring the coffee while waiting to hear the conversation. Mabel was able to reach her husband on his cell phone.

"Honey, I have a question. I found one of those fancy cell phones with all those buttons in my purse. Is this your phone?"

"Heck no, I have my phone with me," her husband replied. "What's going on Mabel?"

"For the life of me, I can't figure out how this phone got in my purse."

"I can't help you with that situation dear. Your guess is as good as mine."

Another phone was ringing in the background where her husband was.

Mabel looked in my direction and told me her husband doesn't know anything about the cell phone. Mabel was still perplexed.

"My husband wouldn't use a phone like this. It doesn't make sense."

"Mabel, that is the security company on the other line. The alarm at the house is going off."

"Oh no," said Mabel.

"Don't worry...okay. I'll call you later."

"Okay," said Mabel.

Then she ended the call with her husband. Mabel and I stared at each other in silence as we sipped our coffee. Someone in the cafeteria dropped a fork on the floor which broke the awkward silence.

Mabel said, "So, tell me about this Frank guy that you were telling me about. You know...the one that's a cop."

I put the cup on the table, looked up at the ceiling, and got my thoughts together.

"Well, like I said, he and the New Jersey police questioned Daymon thoroughly and talked to Daymon's neighbors and co-workers. The police searched Daymon's house and his car. Frank and I searched my sister's apartment in Maryland. While at my sister's apartment, the police in Maryland knocked on a few doors in the building where my sister lived to ask if anyone had seen or heard anything unusual. Of course, they came up empty handed. Daymon cooperated with the police. He had an alibi."

I looked to my left and watched the people in the cafeteria come and go as I drifted into deep thought. I looked at Mabel with tears in my eyes. "No one knows how Morgan disappeared," I sobbed and slapped my hand on the table creating a loud noise. People looked in our direction to see what the commotion was all about.

Mabel stretched her arms across the table to console me. Kim grasped Mabel's hand and started praying, "God grant us the serenity to accept the things we cannot change; courage to change the things we can; and wisdom to know the difference."

Mabel continued the prayer by saying, "Living one day at a time; Enjoying one moment at a time; Accepting hardships as the pathway to peace; Taking, as Jesus did, this sinful world as it is, not as we would have it; Trusting that you will make all things right if we surrender to your will; That we may be reasonably happy in this life forever in the next. Amen."

I gained my composure, sat up straight in my seat, and wiped the tears from my eyes with one of the napkins that I brought to the table.

Mabel said, "I'm here for you."

She went in her purse and pulled out a pen. She took one of the napkins that was on the table and began to write her name and phone number on the napkin. Mabel handed the napkin to me and put the pen back into her purse and said, "I'm going to get back to my side of town. I think we've been here long enough."

"Thanks for listening," I said.

"That's what we need from time to time. I'm here for you. I'm just a phone call away Kim."

"How long does it take you to get home Mabel?"

"Oh...4 or 5 hours."

"What about you?"

"About 3 hours. I can make it home quicker if I put the pedal to the medal."

Mabel said, "No need to speed. Young people are always in a rush to get somewhere nowadays. Remember to slow down and take the scenic route from time to time."

"I plan to do just that," I replied.

Mabel took the phone off the table and put it in her purse.

I said, "What are you going to do with that?"

"Give it to my husband."

"Oh...okay. I'm going out to eat with a friend and get her up to speed on the investigation."

Mabel stood up and pointed at her purse. "That's it!"

"What?" I had no idea what Mabel was talking about.

"That's it! The last time I had this purse with me, Gene was visiting with Daymon. Gene was in a good mood that day because he gave us some money and a gift card to go out to eat that night."

"Do you think he put the phone in your bag?"

"I don't know," Mabel replied.

I looked at the phone, then looked at the purse Mabel was holding, then my eyes went back to Mabel.

"You look like you're in deep thought child."

"I want that phone."

"Why...what are you going to do with it?"

"Mabel, think about what you just said! The last time you had the purse in your possession, Gene was around. What if that's Gene's phone? What if there's some information like a text or a phone call or an email on this phone that will shed some light on this investigation. What if Gene had something to do with my sister's disappearance. I don't know if she is dead or trapped in the basement of someone's house. There might be something on that phone that can answer some questions."

"I can get a charger for this phone. What's Gene's phone number?"

I quickly looked in her purse for the pen that she had. She looked at me like I was crazy for digging in her purse. But she knew what I was doing and why I was doing it.

"You're going to give the phone to the police?" Mabel asked.

"I am going to give it to Frank and the other detective. So, what's the number?"

"I don't know. The number I had for him doesn't work anymore."

"Okay, let's see how far I get with this. I'll be in touch."

I whisked out of the hospital to my car to see if the cell phone charger in my car would fit the phone. I got close to my black BMW 528i, reached into my purse and grabbed my keys. I pressed the button to unlock the doors, then I jumped in and pressed the ignition button to start the car. I pulled out the car charger that was in the glove box. I examined the phone and the phone charger with great scrutiny. Then I inserted the phone charger into the phone to allow it to charge. After that, I closed the car door and proceeded to put the car in gear. I slowly drove off into the traffic that was around the hospital.

At the stop light, I shouted, "Call Frank" and the hands-free mechanism in my car dialed Frank's number. The phone rang twice before Frank answered the phone.

"Hello."

"Hey Frank, I have Gene's cell phone."

"Who?"

"Gene. It's Daymon's lover."

"Really," he said in a surprised tone.

"Yeah, I don't know the passcode for the phone, and I need to charge it. The battery is low."

"Kim, where are you right now?"

"I'm leaving the hospital where Daymon is."

"Is he still alive?"

"Yes, he's unconscious but alive. Frank, do you know anyone who can unlock this phone?"

"Let me talk to a few people and I'll see what they say. Do you know his birth date or address or any significant info?"

"No, but I think I know someone who does."

"Great, I'll call you back."

"Okay Frank, I'll talk to you later."

I accelerated onto the highway to meet my friend at the restaurant as I strapped on my seat belt and headed into the fast lane.

I was staying at a hotel in Jersey City and my friend Tammy just so happened to call me that morning to check on me. She was in Brooklyn visiting her cousin. We decided to meet in the middle at a restaurant in Lower Manhattan.

I used the GPS to navigate a route to the restaurant. When I arrived, I parked near the restaurant, got my things together and glanced at my watch which displayed 6:38pm. I contemplated bringing the phone inside. I didn't want to try to figure out the passcode while ignoring my friend. So, I decided to leave the phone in the car. I disconnected it from the charger and put them both in the glove box. I took a moment to get myself together, then I walked into the restaurant. There was a crowd of college students exiting the restaurant. I held the door open for them. Once I had the opportunity, I gracefully walked toward the podium where the hostess was. I was wearing a pair of tight blue jeans, a black V-neck shirt, and black Reebok sneakers that showed that I was not out to look cute with my slim physique and black hair down to my shoulders. It was more for comfort.

"I'm looking for a friend who is seated somewhere in the restaurant."

The hostess nodded her head to give me the okay to roam around the restaurant while she looked at the chart of available tables. I strolled by the bar and Tammy stood up by a table and waved her hand in a motion to get me to walk in her direction. I gave her a warm embrace before sitting down on one of the chairs. Tammy looked at me and noticed the bags under my eyes.

"Are you getting enough rest? You look tired girl. I know times are rough right now."

The waiter came with the appetizers and wine that Tammy previously ordered and placed them on the table. We ordered the entrees and continued to talk.

I looked at Tammy with disbelief. "No one knows where Morgan is. The police have no leads and Morgan's boyfriend is in a coma. He did cooperate with the police, but it doesn't make sense. The day I followed him was the day he got into the accident. He realized I was following him. Why did he try to get away from me? What is he hiding?"

"What? I don't remember you telling me that." Tammy replied.

"I thought I did. The last time we spoke, you had just got back from the cruise."

"That was two weeks ago. We were with your trainer. You were talking to him for a long time...remember? We worked out together that day. His name is Kelvin...right?"

Tammy said, "Calvin." "Oh yeah, I was distracted at the end of the workout that day when we were at his gym. I saw one of his clients arguing with someone on the phone as she was leaving. She was very loud. It didn't make any sense for her to be that loud out in public. So, refresh my memory. What happened in New Jersey?"

"Oh yeah, I do remember there was a lot of commotion in the back by the exit that day. Anyway, I followed Daymon on the day of his accident. He knew I was following him. He was trying to get away from me by driving faster, but I'll get back to that part.

The police checked Daymon's phone records and found a few numbers. The day Morgan went missing, Daymon had called a guy named Gene, short for Eugene, and Gene was one of Daymon's alibis."

"Daymon said he was home alone that day. That guy Gene stopped by to see Daymon. The neighbors said they saw the Range Rover, which was Gene's, at Daymon's house and they did not see anything unusual."

"No one recalls seeing Morgan's car at Daymon's house. I spoke to Morgan before she disappeared. She told me she was going to his house a day early to show off her new hair style and to discuss moving in with him since they were getting closer and having a long-distance relationship. That was around 6 pm on a Saturday. That was the last time I spoke to Morgan. Gene died before I got a chance to talk to him."

"Damn! Really, what happened? How did he die?"

"You are not going to believe this! Better yet, take a guess girl!"

"He died while having sex?"

I laughed so hard. "No, try again."

"Suicide?"

"His condo caught on fire.  He was in his condo when it exploded into flames."

"Sounds like foul play to me girl."

"You better believe it.  After I got the information from Frank, the detective, I went to the condo in New Jersey to see if the neighbors saw Morgan there.  I know the police did their part, but my sister is still missing.  That's why I feel the need to get involved in the detective work."

"I hear ya, Colombo.  I would get involved too.  But you're doing a lot of traveling back and forth to New Jersey.  You're going to wear yourself out."

"If that's what it takes to get some answers...so be it."  Tammy nodded her head in agreement.  "It's hard to imagine that my sister is locked up in a basement getting raped every day or believing that she's dead and her body is in the woods waiting for the animals to devour her limb by limb."  I cringed and balled up my fist under the table.

The waiter came to the table with our meals and placed the plates on the table. Steam was coming from the food.

The waiter said, "The plates are very hot, please be careful."

We thanked him and prepared to eat our food. We glanced at the basketball game on the TV then sat in silence for a while.

Tammy took her glass of wine and said, "I believe you will find the answers to your questions. You are going to find your sister. I know you put 110% into whatever you get involved in. If you need anything...money, a place to stay, anything, let me know." We picked up their glasses and made a toast to that statement and drank our wine. I stared at Tammy and smiled with gratitude.

"How is life as a baller?"

I asked as she cut the salmon to taste it. The mashed potatoes and broccoli were also on her plate along with the appetizers that were on the table. I sampled the appetizers while waiting for a response from her.

Tammy shook her head from side-to-side and looked up at the ceiling.

"Since my co-workers and I won the lottery, I feel secure financially. I'm aware that people want to get their hands on the money. Banks call me trying to persuade me to invest in CDs, Mutual Funds, and the like. I took care of my parents, of course, and bought my brother a barber shop. He's doing well. He's going to open another barber shop once he finds a good location. My sister and her crew are the ones that are really acting like they are entitled to the money I won. I bought my sister a car and gave her some cash. They always come around with a new business idea that they want me to invest in."

"How much did you all win again?"

"There were 13 of us and we each walked away with just about eleven million dollars after taxes. I still talk to most of my co-workers. We discuss different investment options, places we've been, influential people we've met. It's like an investor's club."

"Tell me what happen when you were in New Jersey knocking on doors Colombo."

Tammy switched the subject. They both laughed and that gave Tammy time to eat her meal. Kim put her fork down and drank some wine to wash down the food in her mouth.

"I knocked on a few doors and none of the neighbors saw my sister. One guy gave up some good info when I knocked on his door. He lived in the building directly across from Gene's place. When I spoke to the guy, I thought he was kind of cute. He was in shape. He answered the door shirtless with sunglasses on. His condo was clean, but it smelled like he was smoking weed or just finished smoking."

"What did you think of him?"

"He was attractive. He had a few nice tattoos, but girl his breath was kickin' and he had a tattoo on his neck. It was some type of logo or symbol. I didn't get a good look at it, but he was not my type."

"I showed him a picture of Morgan and asked him if he'd seen her. Then, I asked him what he knew about Gene. He told me that Gene was respectable and had a lot of girlfriends."

I started to mimic the guy I was talking about. I made my voice sound deeper. "I think he goes both ways. I've seen him act metro sexual around me. Shit, I think he was gay. Let's call a spade a spade. Let me see that picture again.  Nah, I don't remember seeing her with him."

I switched back to my regular voice.  "He said it just like that.  Like he was real cool and tough."

"He did mention that Gene was a smoker. Oh...this's what he said."  I switched back to my manly voice.

"I wasn't here when it happened.  To come back home and find out the nigga's place exploded, that was some wild shit."

"Then, he slowly glanced at my body from top to bottom and stared into my eyes and asked, Are you a cop?  Nah, you're way too sexy to be cop."  Tammy started laughing at the way I portrayed the guy.

I gave him a smirk and said, "No, I'm just a lawyer looking for my sister.  I think that explosion had something to do with my sister's disappearance but thank you for the compliment and thank you for your time."

"I immediately turned around and left because he did not have much info to give me after that.  I didn't want to waste any more time. I went to a few more condos, at least 4, and no one opened the door.  This was on a

Saturday, so maybe they were out shopping or
running errands. Luckily, as I was leaving
the building, there was a woman who lived
near Gene's condo in the next building which
had another set of 12 condos or more. I
practically jogged over to her as she was
headed into her building."

"As I got closer, I noticed she was wearing
scrubs when she emerged from her car. You
can tell she was in the medical field. She
had her hair in a ponytail. She looked
young, maybe in her late twenties. She drove
a Mercedes coupe and she was pulling a
briefcase with wheels. She was holding some
mail and magazines. She stopped walking and
tried to put that stuff in the briefcase that
was full of papers and folders. I didn't
know if she was a nurse, a doctor, or a
medical student. I got her attention as she
turned on the car alarm."

"Excuse me!  Hello."

"I'm not interested."  She replied and
started to walk away.

I pulled out the photograph of Morgan.  "I'm
not selling anything."

"Have you seen this female?"

"She stopped and gave me a moment of her time. She extended her hand and took the photograph out of my hand. She paused and stared at the photograph of Morgan."

"She looks familiar...I've seen her before."

"You have! Did you know Gene?"

"Eugene? Yeah, I know about Gene. Who are you?"

"My name is Kim, and this is a picture of my sister, Morgan. She's been missing for three weeks. To tell you the truth, the explosion at Gene's place had something to do with her disappearance."

"Oh yeah! That was a shame. Gene was a good guy, sort of like a girlfriend, you know he was gay...right?"

"Yes, I found out about that."

"You know a condo just doesn't explode in flames. Do you agree?"

"Yeah. Tell me what you know about the explosion."

We slowly began to walk to the entrance of the building where the female lived.

"Someone set him up is what I think, and Gene knew what happened to my sister. The only other person I know that can answer my questions about my sister's disappearance is in a coma. Do you know where Gene was last Saturday?"

"No, I don't hang with him that much. The only thing I can tell you is that Gene lost his sense of smell. If there was a gas leak in his condo, I'm not sure he would smell it."

They were standing by the steps of the building. The female gave a look like she had a long day, and she had no more information to give. I opened my purse and put the picture back in it and pulled out one of my business cards.

"Look, take my card. Give me a call if you hear anything or if you can remember anything else."

She took the time to read every word on the card. She quickly looked up and said, "Oh, you're a lawyer."

Then she asked, "Are the police helping you with your investigation?"

"Yes, but no one said anything about Gene not being able to smell."

I looked away and stared at the grass while I pondered on that thought. The female had an epiphany, and it snapped me back to reality.

"I remember now. I remember seeing your sister's face on the news. I hope you find her. I have a sister too. I would probably do the same thing you're doing if she came up missing."

I waved goodbye as I took out my cell phone and called Frank to give him an update.

"Frank any news about what happened at Gene's condo?"

"Not yet. The place was burned up pretty bad and it is going to take a while for them to finish the investigation. We searched through the phone records, and we noticed that there were no calls made from his cell phone nor to his cell phone two days after you talked to your sister. I wish I had more information for you, but it's been three weeks, and we have no leads. We've checked with the coroner's offices and medical examiners in Maryland and New Jersey. We asked about their Jane Doe cases and we came up with nothing. Can you gather a list of friends and places that Morgan frequented? We can double check our findings and make sure we Leave no stone unturned."

"I'll do what I can to help you. If you want a private investigator, I can help you find one. I won't let you down. I owe it to your father. He was a good friend of mine! I watched you and your sister grow up. You're like family to me. I'll keep searching even if this case is deemed a cold case."

"Thank you, Frank!"

"No problem, Kim! I'll stay in touch. Take care."

"I slowly walked to my car. I examined everything around me from the condos to the entrance of each building that was in eyesight of Gene's condo. On the way to my car, I could hear the sound of music and the aroma of food was in the air. When I looked around, I couldn't tell which direction it was coming from. I got to my car and was able to see the damage the explosion caused to Gene's condo from where I was standing. I stood there in disbelief, asking myself, how did all of this happen."

Tammy shook her head.

"Damn girl!  That was one hell of a story."

We ate in silence for a while, then we started talking about other people that we knew and the issues they were dealing with. After the meal, I got my stuff together.  We hugged each other for a long time.

"Call me whenever you need me, Kim!  We're sisters for life."

"I know.  Thanks!  I really need people in my corner right now."

"You got one right here."

"Well, I'm going to get on the road.  When are you going home?"

"Tomorrow.  I'll leave New York while people are at work.  There shouldn't be that much traffic after rush hour."

While I was traveling back to Maryland to prepare myself for the upcoming work week, I pondered on the details of the conversations I had with the two people I spoke to.  I was struggling with the fact that Morgan might be dead.  When I was driving down the New Jersey

Turnpike, I was thinking really hard. If I could find out what happened at the condo, I might have a better understanding of what happened to Morgan.

Meanwhile, Tammy was making plans to have dinner with her personal trainer back in Maryland. They decided to meet the next day for dinner. At a restaurant, Calvin ordered a drink to get the dinner started. It was happy hour, and the restaurant was very busy. There were people there who just got off from work and some people were there just to watch the sport events that were going to be aired on TV. Calvin began to tell Tammy how thankful he was for all the referrals she had given him, which increased his clientele.

Calvin asked, "So what's been up with you?"

She replied, "I sold the third property that I was rehabbing. The seminars and the circle of investors have been a great asset. It takes money to make money. That's the truth. The process seems to be straight forward so far. A few problems here and there, but I'm gettin' it done. I have a close friend that is a realtor. She helps me find the properties and negotiate the deal. My contractor has a crew that does whatever needs to be done. If I have any issues, I tell the investment group about the issues with the property.  The people in the group always have the resources to get things done. Pretty soon, I'll be able to purchase multi-unit properties."

"Hopefully, I can find a four unit property and find some good renters.  Who knows.  I have a good eye for making properties look good with curb appeal.  I keep bringing deals and ideas to the table."

"So, the contractors are lovin' me right now because I'm putting money in their pockets. The Realtor is getting her commission, and I'm paying the membership fees to use the investment groups' resources."

"You know, lawyers, short sell specialists, whatever is needed.  Somebody knows someone who has the contact.  What about you?  How was that trip to Atlantic City?"

"It was tight," Calvin replied.

He took a sip of his Mojito and leaned in closer to talk because it was getting noisy in the restaurant.

"I took my girl to her first boxing match. We had great seats.  There were a lot of fights before the main event."

Tammy asked, "Who was the main event?"

"Bernard Hopkins and some other guy I never heard of."

The waiter arrived. He asked, "Y'all ready to order. I see you are almost ready for a refill sir."

Tammy looked at Calvin. Calvin gave a quick smile and said, "Let's keep the party going. You know I'm not going to say no."

The waiter nodded his head and began to take their order. He looked at Tammy first.

"I'll take a mojito, hummus with the pita, and a salmon salad."

The waiter looked at Calvin. "Okay! What about you? What would you like to have?"

"I'll take the crab soup, the lobster roll, and another mojito."

"Okay! I'll get started on the drinks and the appetizers." The waiter walked off to tend to the other patrons.

"Hey, you know what? You're the first person to know about this. I'm ready to start my own business. Get my own training facility up and running. I got the experience.

I know some people that would be a good fit to work with me and train the clients. I think I have enough clientele, thanks to you. Since you spoke about your investment group and how you find properties, how about helping me find a spot for my gym? My own personal gym!"

"What are you going to call it?"

"Excel Workout Studio."

"Okay big baller! I'll look out for you, but you have to do some of the legwork and keep your eyes open too. Look around and let me know if you see a good property. Who knows, we might be able to work something out where we both make a profit. You know what I'm about? Money and happiness!"

The waiter came to the table with their appetizers and the drinks.

"Wow, that was fast!" Tammy said.

"Yeah, Razzle is cool like that. That's why I like this restaurant." Calvin said.

The waiter smiled ear to ear.

"I'll be back shortly with the food. Enjoy!"

Tammy and Calvin raised their drinks and made a toast to their business venture.

Ding dong. Meanwhile, the doorbell rang at Tammy's house. Tammy's husband Steve was watching the news when Tammy's friend came to the house. Steve got up to open the door.

"Hey Steve, good to see you. I came by to see Tammy real quick."

"She's not here."

"Oh, okay I'll call her cell phone. Normally she would be home around this time."

Steve let Tammy's friend in. She was standing in the foyer when Steve said, "Hold on I'll call her right now."

Steve walked to the kitchen to get the cordless phone. He called Tammy and she answered the phone while she was still out with Calvin.

"Hello."

"Leslie is here. Where are you?"

"Razzle. Do you want me to bring you something to eat?"

"Nah, I'm good. Hold on." Steve passed the phone to Leslie.

"She's at Razzle," he said.

Leslie stood in the foyer with the cordless phone and asked, "You're at Razzle? Who you with?"

"Calvin."

"The trainer? Oh, you worked out today."

Steve was caught off guard when he heard that. He began to think Tammy was up to no good. Leslie sat on the steps in the foyer and Steve paced around the kitchen getting filled with anger by the minute. Steve tried to stay calm while Leslie was there. He took a deep breath and poured a glass of water into a cup.

Leslie finished her conversation with Tammy and walked into the kitchen to give Steve the cordless phone.

Steve asked Leslie, "Who is she with?"

"Calvin," she said.

His facial expression changed. He frowned as he reached for the phone that Leslie was passing to him. Steve was getting mad, and Leslie noticed it.

She said, "Oh don't trip off of that! It's just Calvin."

Steve knew that this could turn into something more than a personal trainer and client workout relationship.

Leslie turned around and threw her hand in the air as she walked toward the door.

"I'll see ya later."

"Alright, see ya Leslie."

She stopped to let Steve open the door. Steve walked to the door, opened it, and watched Leslie walk to her car. Steve was thinking to himself. Damn, Leslie has a nice body. How would Tammy feel if I was having dinner with Leslie without her knowing about it?

His mind began to wander about all the things that had been done without him knowing about it. He called Tammy back.

Before she could say hello, Steve asked,

"Who's at the restaurant with you?"

She confirmed that she was out with Calvin. Steve immediately ended the call. His blood began to boil. He was wondering how many times they had hooked up. How many times have they had sex? Did they have sex in their house when they were supposed to be working out?

# CHAPTER 3

## KIM

I made it home. I put my leather duffel bag by the steps. That's when I realized my stomach was growling. So, I went to the kitchen and found some leftover baked chicken and a container of salad in the refrigerator. I grabbed the salad dressing to complete the quick meal. When I went upstairs to get my clothes together for the next day, I got my paperwork organized and took a shower. The shower was nice and hot, just the way I like it. I thought about Daymon's involvement in this matter.

Why did he take off the way he did when he noticed me in his neck of the woods?

Why did Gene go down south to see his aunt who's related to a man who owns a funeral home?

Is there any useful info on that phone that Mabel gave me?

Why and how did Gene's place explode?

Those thoughts ran through my mind over and over again. After a long hot shower, I dried myself off, laid down, then went to sleep naked. I had a dream that night. My sister was naked, chained to a bed with two men standing around masturbating while waiting for the third guy to finish raping her. I woke up screaming and crying because it seemed too real. It was a dream that I would never forget. I rolled out of bed and got on my knees to pray.

"Where is Morgan GOD? Please prepare me for the worst and bless me with better days. I need your help to make it through this. Please help me find my sister and keep the rest of my family safe. I can do all things through Christ. I believe that to be true. This is my prayer. In Jesus name...Amen."

The night was coming to an end with the morning sun making its presents known. I didn't get any work done that night. I turned on the TV and sat still on the edge of the bed. I flipped through the channels and found Harlem Nights playing. It would be nice to have a good laugh right now, I thought to myself. After watching about thirty minutes of the movie, I decided to get dressed and head into the office early.

My alarm clock went off at 5:00am. I changed the channel to watch the morning news. My cell phone was ringing, but I misplaced the phone. I followed the sound to the bathroom. The phone stopped ringing by the time I found it. The phone rang again while I was scrolling through the phone.

"Hello."

"Hey, good morning, sunshine. You sound wide awake."

"Hey Lawrence. Normally, I would still be sleeping. I like to get all my beauty rest."

"I miss you."

"I miss you, too."

"How did the funeral arrangements turn out?"

"Death is always a hard pill to swallow, but yeah, there were some problems."

"My mother's skin looked darker than usual, and they put too much powder on her. The funeral service went well, without a hitch. No one dropped the casket and there was plenty of food."

"That's not funny Lawrence."

"I know, I just wanted to lighten the mood. But for real, my uncle tripped over something on the way to the grave site.  It could have turned ugly real quick."

"Okay, you are such a fool sometimes.  But seriously, how are you doing?"

"It's hard to smile right now.  I know I've been quiet, and you haven't heard from me that much.  When my mother called and told me she couldn't breathe, I couldn't get to her quick enough.  I couldn't get anyone over there either.  We were in Richmond implementing a network solution for my client when it happened."

"My guys took care of everything in my absence.  Today, I added one more device. Then I cleaned up, talked to the client, and now I'm on the road."

There was a brief silence.  Lawrence sighed and continued talking.

"She died because I was too far away.  My dad is gone.  So, she had no one there to help her.  I was thinking she should've had one of those necklaces with the remote so she could press the button and get some help.  She told me she was always tired and said she would manage. She would tell me it was just part of getting old. My emotions and my attitude are all over the place. I was in Virginia at her condo looking at all the stuff we have to move out. What's been going on with you? I'm tired of talking about what I went through. To tell you the truth, I just want to get away. I'm trying to deal with the fact that I don't have parents anymore."

"Babe, I'm sorry that you're going through this. Both of us are having a rough time right now. Where are you? I want you to come over."

"I thought you would never ask. I was going to surprise you. I'm right around the corner."

"Oh yeah!"

"I'm in your neighborhood."

"I can't wait to see you."

Lawrence slowly drove through her neighborhood until he reached her street. He sped up with a little urgency, then he pulled into the driveway of her townhouse. Lawrence got out of the white Cadillac Escalade and calmly walked to the front door. He was an average size dark skin man with a muscular

stature, a strong hair line, and a well-
trimmed beard.

I looked in the mirror, grabbed my silk robe
and put on some lip gloss.  He used his keys
to unlock the door.  I heard the chime from
the alarm system when he opened the door.  I
went downstairs and greeted Lawrence with a
big smile.  I turned on the light in the
foyer and gave him a hug and a long seductive
kiss.  I was holding his hand leading the way
into the kitchen.

I grabbed the empty tea kettle that was by
the sink, filled it up with water, and put it
on the stove to heat up the water for some
morning tea.

Lawrence asked, "Are you hungry babe?
I can make an egg and cheese sandwich with
some bacon on the side."

I looked at him and smiled with love in my
eyes.  "You always like cooking for me."

"That's not the only thing I like doing for
you."

"What else do you like doing for me?"

"I like to be the shoulder you can lean on; I

like supporting you, and I like lending you, my ear. In other words, I'm a good listener."

"Yes, you are!"

"Also, I like to make you moan."

"What?"

That statement caught me off guard. But it made me exhale with anticipation of getting sexual. I stood there watching him walk toward me. He stood behind me and gave me a hug. He moved my hair to the side and whispered in my ear.

"I need you more each day. I can't stop thinking about you. You're my lover. Let me love you."

He gently squeezed my breast as he hugged me from behind. I turned around and kissed him passionately. He caressed me, kissed me all over my neck, and started to undress me. He untied the robe I was wearing a let it drop to the kitchen floor. Lawrence seductively bent me over the kitchen counter. I began to spread my legs. He pushed his pants and boxers down to his ankles. Then he put his erection to use between my thighs. He continued to rub, kiss, and touch every inch of me until I was moist.  I looked back at him erotically.

"Show me how much you need me."

He slapped my ass and got on his knees to spread my butt cheeks and commenced cunnilingus to get the escapade started.  I started breathing harder.  Four minutes into it, I started moving to the rhythm of his tongue.  He stood up behind me and slowly entered me.  Lawrence stood still for a moment to enjoy the view of my slim body, manicured nails, and natural hair positioned over the granite countertop.  He put his hands on my shoulder and gave me every inch of what I like.

"Ooouuu!"

"Yeah babe, that's what I like to hear.  Let me go a little deeper."

"Ooouuu!"

My legs quivered.  Then the tea kettle started to whistle.  He kept going but faster and harder for seven minutes.  I pushed my ass toward him to intensify the feeling.  My body started to shake, and Lawrence went faster.  He pulled out and ejaculated all over my back. He waddled over to the sink to get a few paper towels to wipe me clean. The kettle was still whistling. Lawrence wiped my back until my back was dry. I moved closer to the stove to turn the burner off. My loving eyes were watching him. He wiped himself clean, stepped out of his pants and boxers, and left them on the dark wood floor in the kitchen. He walked to the living room to sit on the couch with nothing but his socks and a shirt on. I walked over to the living room where he was and sat on his lap and started to grind on him to get him aroused again. While on the couch, soft moans and heavy breathing echoed in the living room. Eleven minutes go by, and Lawrence grabbed a firm grip of my ass and started thrusting deeper into me. I gave him what he wanted and started riding him faster until my body started shaking as I climaxed again. Lawrence kept going while I was having an orgasm. He got closer to my ear.

"I love you, Kim."

He stood up from the couch with his muscular arms wrapped around me. I was worried that he was going to drop me. So, I wrapped my arms around his neck and held on for dear life as we continued to go at it again.

He held my body, and I wrapped her legs around him. After about 40 strokes, he laid me on the couch and was giving it to me in the missionary position. Suddenly, I opened my legs as wide as I could to resemble the letter V, and he pulled out and ejaculated on body again. He stood up and stared at my naked body.

"Come closer handsome."

I sucked on his erection to make sure he was satisfied. He was out of breath and smiling with pleasure. He took off his polo shirt and then used his T-shirt to clean off my stomach. We laid on the couch naked and cuddled like a loving couple.

"I was planning to go to work today, but you put it on me and now I feel lazy."

Lawrence grinned when he heard what I said.

"What are you doing today handsome?"

"Well, I'm going to my place to unpack, check the mail, return some phone calls, and figure out what needs to be done when I go back to work on Wednesday. I'll come back later if you are going out. I'll be staying here with you since we haven't seen each other for a month, and I know you need the company."

"Yes, I need all the support I can get. I've been absent from work too. I'll go in late, and I can meet you back here in a few hours. I need to have someone hold me at night. I had a bad dream last night. That's why I was up so early."

"No problem babe. I'll be your confidant. What was your dream about?"

"Morgan. She was trying to tell me something while she was getting raped, but I didn't understand what she was saying. She had blood on her clothes. She fell to the ground in front of me while the guys ran away. She was unconscious. I was trying to get her up and I was screaming for help. I was screaming so loud; I woke myself up."

"Damn! I'm here now. I'll calm your nerves."

They both smiled. Lawrence looked at his watch.

"Oh damn, it's almost 8 o'clock."

"Come on. Let's take a shower. I have to go to the office, and you can have some free time for yourself."

I stood up, grabbed his hand, and led him to the stairs. He stopped at the bottom of the stairs to watch me walk upstairs.

I turned around and started blushing.

"What?"

"Nothing. I just want to see you walk. I have not seen your naked body in a month. Go ahead, keep walking!"

I was in a good mood, so I gave him a show.

Moving slowly up the stairs, I seduced him with my moves. My movements mimicked those of a show girl in Las Vegas enticing the men in the crowd. Lawrence stood and smiled as he started to get another erection.

Just then, the phone rang. I moved up the stairs a little quicker when I heard my cell phone ringing in the bathroom. I answered the call.

"Hello?"

"Hey K, I need to talk to you. Let me tell you what happened last night."

"Hold up Tammy! I have to jump in the shower, Lawrence is over here, and I had planned on going to the office to help my colleague with a case. I'm not quite ready to take on a new case in court right now. However, bills need to be paid, and I can't be a lawyer unless I practice law."

"Is everything okay?"

"Girl, Steve is trippin' but, okay girl, call me later."

"Okay."

I looked at the clock and started thinking. Damn, I already made a commitment to help with this case. If I can make it out of here before 9:00am, I won't have to deal with that much traffic.

Lawrence had the water running and had just turned on some music. I put the phone on the vanity and stepped into the shower. Lawrence and I gazed in each other's eyes while Lawrence bathed me and then bathed himself. When I rinsed the soap off my body, we embraced and held each other under the warm shower water and danced slowly to a song that was playing. The steam filled the bathroom. We had a silent moment while we stood in the shower holding each other.

When the song was over, I said, "Babe, I have

to go."

Lawrence sighed. "I know."

We danced in silence while the next song played. Not a word was uttered. At that moment, I realized the load I had to carry with my sister missing was heavy. All the while, I knew I still had to conduct myself as a strong studious woman in corporate America. The song ended and I kissed Lawrence passionately and got out of the shower. I grabbed my towel and headed to the bed to put lotion on, grab a bra, and a pair of matching panties. I looked at the window and noticed the orange glow from the morning sun shining through the blinds. It was almost 9:00am.

I chose to wear my tan business dress suit, matching tan heels and a white blouse. Lawrence was clean, but he was wearing the same clothes that he had on earlier. I made my way downstairs. He met me in the kitchen and gave me another hug.

I gazed into his eyes. "I'll get with you later. We can do all the touching and hugging you want when I get back."

He frowned. "Are you rushing me out of here?"

I smiled. "Yes, I have to go to the office. There shouldn't be that much traffic going to the city right now, but you never know."

"I hear ya."

We both took some time to clean up the kitchen.

Lawrence picked up his T-shirt and my robe.

He stood and admired my body while he watched me pack my bag with some healthy snacks. After that, he sat down and put his shoes on.

"You know you can cook whatever you want while you're here."

"Nah, I'm going straight home. I'll be there in no time. I'll eat when I get there. You smell good!"

"Thank you!"

I grabbed a bottle of water and started walking toward the front door.

"You're sure you don't want something to eat Lawrence?"

He grinned. "Are you cooking? If you are,

I'll take some pancakes and eggs!"

"You're crazy. Do you want an egg sandwich or some fruit? I'm not making any pancakes. I ain't got time for that."

"Nah, I'm good...well give me one of those apples and some water. You got me feeling dehydrated after putting in that work!"

We both laughed.

"Boy, you're silly."

I walked quickly to get the apple from the fridge. I tossed it to him and watched him walk over to the sink to wash it off. I paused to make sure I had my car keys, my black Gucci tote, my wallet, and my laptop bag that was by the front door. Walking over to the bathroom, I glanced at Lawrence to see if he was ready. In the bathroom, I put lotion on my hands and applied some lip gloss. Just then, Lawrence moved toward the bathroom. He was leaning on the door frame of the bathroom staring at my reflection in the mirror.

"You're fine! God didn't make any mistakes when he made you."

"I like all the attention and the complements boo.  You sure do stare a lot.  Do you know that?"

We shared a quick laugh.

"You deserve it!"

"I love you, Kim."

I froze then turned to face him.

"What did you say?  You love me?"

"Life is precious and short.  I love spending time with you.  I love seeing you.  I love you!"

I kissed his lips softly to cherish the moment.

"I must have put it on you," I said.

"Yes, you did!  I needed that to bring me back to reality.  Death was all round me.
The funeral had me down.  You made me forget about all that for a little while.  We have to enjoy this time, this life, these moments.
You know what I mean?"

"Yeah, you're getting serious on me early in the morning?  Right now, I'm numb and I need support. I feel happy one minute, then the next minute, I break down."

Tears started to come down my face.

"I don't know what happened to my sister."

I fell into his arms weeping. He held me tightly.

"Let it all out babe. I'm here for you."

I looked in his eyes. "I need you to come back here tonight."

"No doubt. You're going through it too. I'm gonna be here for you. You don't have endure all of this on your own."

I looked in the mirror to make sure I had my composure together. I wiped my face and picked up my purse to head out the door.

Lawrence was right behind me. I grabbed the laptop bag and turned on the security alarm. We walked outside to see the sun shining on everything around us. After locking the front door, I reached for his hand. I got close to his ear and whispered, "I love you too." Then, I got in my car to drive to work.

Lawrence stood there with a smile on his face like a little kid with a birthday cake in his eyesight. He walked to his SUV and watched me drive off. I beeped the horn to say goodbye.

I was on my way to the law firm in the District of Columbia where I worked as a real estate lawyer.

I got in the elevator at the office, pressed the button for the twelfth floor, and started to think about some files I needed to review before the client showed up at our reputable private practice downtown near the main tourist attractions and museums in DC. The chime of the elevator could be heard throughout the office space. I got off on my floor and noticed the secretary's computer was on, but she was nowhere to be found. My colleague was walking out of one of the offices. She greeted me with her arms stretched wide. We embraced like old friends.

"Kim, how are you? Did the police get any leads?"

"No, not yet. The suspect is still in a comma. He should be able to fill in the blanks when he comes to. We have a cell phone from a second suspect.

The police are trying to extract the data from the phone to see if there's any useful info they can use to find Morgan.  I have someone working on that.  I should call him today."

The feeling of depression took over my mood, I looked down and shook my head in disbelief. I quickly changed the subject and got my composure together.

"What's going on with your case Daniel?"

"Well, my client has a commercial property and the AC unit on top of the building isn't working.  The client is leasing, and the landlord of the building is not willing to help cover the charges to get a new unit installed on top of the building."

I asked, "Why won't the landlord pay for the new unit?"

"My client said the landlord told him he was at the end of the lease and since my client wasn't going to renew his lease, the landlord did not think it was necessary.  Therefore, it did not seem to be a good business deal to the landlord."

"I see.  So, what's your plan Daniel?"

"Kim, I have a deadline and I know you had a case like this. I need your help with researching the case law and legislation that might be useful for this case. We won't have to spend a lot of time looking for the information that we need."

"Okay Daniel, let me get myself together and I'll let you know when I can review that case with you."

"You're the best Kim. I owe you! Where do you want to go for lunch? It's on me."

I looked in the air and said, "Let's see, Ruth Chris or The Four Seasons."

We both laughed, because both of those restaurants come with an expensive bill to pay when all the food and drinks are gone. Suddenly, my ringing cell phone broke up the laughter. Franks's number showed up on the screen.

"Hello, Frank. Please tell me that you have good news!"

I motioned with my index finger to tell Daniel that I needed a minute alone. Daniel understood and left me to my phone call.

I proceeded to walk to my own office with my laptop bag and purse on my right shoulder and the phone in my left hand.

"We got the data from the phone."

I placed my things in one of the chairs facing my desk. I closed the door and sat down in the other chair to get the details.

"Kim, you won't believe this. Gene made a video. He does confess to hurting someone, but he never mentioned any names. He doesn't say anything about a body. In the video, he says if something happens to him, Daymon is the one with the answers. I'm not saying Morgan is dead. But without a body we can't convict anyone. The explosion at Gene's condo was caused by some type of gas leak. That leaves us in the same position. Gene is dead. Daymon is incapacitated and your sister is still missing."

I was so quiet that Frank could hear the beeping horns from the city traffic through my phone.

"Hello...Kim?"

"Yeah, I'm still here."

"Oh...okay. I'll keep you posted. Keep your head up kiddo."

I walked around my office nervously pacing back and forth. I took the elevator downstairs to get some air.

Standing outside of the building, I stared at the sky and just looked aimlessly trying to figure out what the next step should be. My cell phone rang again. I saw that it was Tammy calling again. I answered the call.

"Hey Tammy, I don't know what to say right now."

"What's wrong, Kim?"

I looked at the cars and the pedestrians passing by. In disbelief, I began to sigh.

"I'm not ready to talk about it."

Tammy said, "I can hear traffic in the background. Where are you on your way to?"

"I'm standing outside trying to gather my thoughts. Sorry for not calling you back. What's going on?"

"Steve did the unthinkable."

"He cheated on you?"

"No girl! He went off on me. He broke my cell phone, and he was acting like he was going to hit me. I was scared. I was looking for something to hit him with. He didn't believe anything I was saying. He went through my phone and looked at the texts between me and Calvin. He saw some pictures that Calvin sent to me and went crazy. He opened the front door and threw the phone on the steps. I've never seen him mad like this. I can hear him cursing right now. I need to get out of here."

"Well, what did you expect Tammy? Tell me something Tee. Did you have sex with him? Did you kiss him or anything like that?"

"No! We've hugged. I've felt his body close to mine, but I didn't fuck him and that's the shit that got me mad. If I was going to get into trouble like this because I had dinner with a male friend, then I should've fucked him. At least it would've been worth it."

"So, you do want to fuck him."

"I thought about it. Yeah, I would not mind getting some from him. When he works out with me, we do jumping jacks sometimes and I can see his dick jumping around in his

basketball shorts. I can't lie, I wanted to
see it...perhaps suck on it, but nothing
happened."

There was a short moment of silence. I
stopped at the corner of the street to think
about what Tammy was saying. Tammy was on a
cordless phone looking at pictures of her and
her husband that were on display in the
living room. Tammy broke the silence.

"But anyway, I'm going to my beach house for
a week. You should come with me this weekend
after work to get your mind off things and
help me plan my escape from Steve before I
kill his ass or before he kills me."

I shook my head from left to right. "You're
trippin' Tee. Besides, I can't go out there
this weekend. Lawrence is coming by tonight.
I have not seen him in a while, and I want to
spend time with him. How far is the beach
house from here anyway?"

"It takes about three hours to get to Shore
Point Drive in Ocean City. I was going to
invite some of the girls. You know, a good
old road trip for old times. But I
understand if you can't make it. You want
some good lovin' from your boo."

"Yeah, I don't want to leave him hanging...you know what I mean."

"All right girl. I'll call to check on you. Oh, any news about Morgan?"

I hesitated and ran my fingers through my hair.

"Ah...no."

"Damn! All right then, I'll check on you later...okay."

"Okay."

I continued my stroll around the busy city area where I worked. I stopped at another corner where I could see my office building from afar. Cars were zooming by, and people were walking on the sidewalk dressed for work or the gym. Some rode bikes or walked their dogs. My stride got slower and slower. Then I stopped.

"No matter what happens, life goes on," I said to myself.

I stood still on the city sidewalk watching all the people moving to and from trying to get to their destination. I walked around a little longer and then went back into the

office building where I work. I walked
through the lobby and headed toward the
elevator. I got on the elevator and sent a
text to Lawrence saying, "I can't wait to see
u later." I got off the elevator, greeted
the receptionist, then strolled to my office.
I looked at the papers and folders that
needed to be reviewed for the upcoming case.

Lawrence texted me back, "Can't wait. I know
exactly what you need for a good night's
rest."

I texted back, "Put it on me tonight."

"No doubt," he replied.

Steve looked at Sherri passionately with his
eyes. I smiled when I noticed I was getting
wet between my legs. I grabbed one of the
folders and started reading.

I quickly went through the documents and
wrote down some notes to give to my coworker
for the upcoming case. I stayed as busy as I
could to stop from thinking about my sister
and the whole ordeal. Folder after
folder, paper after paper, I was like a
working machine. One hour went by. Then
two. Before I knew it, it was starting to
get dark outside.

Five hours had gone by when I glanced at the black and silver clock that was hanging on the neutral-toned wall in my office.

There was a knock on the door accompanied by the sound of beeping horns from the cars in rush hour traffic that drew my attention away from the clock. The office secretary proceeded to walk in. She was sympathetic as she mentioned that she was on her way home.

She stood at the front of my desk and asked, "Are you trying to make up for lost time or do you just love what you do? Which one is it?" I gave a slight smirk.

"No, Cindy, I'm just trying to stay busy in order to stop thinking negative thoughts."

"I understand. Any word about your sister's whereabouts?"

"No, nothing."

I looked out the window to focus on something else to prevent myself from crying.

"You'll get some info soon Kim. Just hang in there."

"I will. Thanks!"

"I'll see ya next week."

"Yes, have a good weekend."

I paused for a minute to reflect on what was said. I worked a little while longer, then I closed my office door and locked it. I folded my arms, leaned back in my chair, and closed my eyes to take a mental break.

The break did not last long because the phone started to ring. It was Daniel.

"How long are you staying tonight?"

"Not long."

"Yeah, I hear ya. I'm on my way to the Third Street Lounge. Care to join me? My treat. I owe you for helping me with this case."

"I'll take a rain check."

"Come on! A female as beautiful as you should not be trapped in the office on a Friday burning the midnight oil."

"I'm fine actually; we'll have another opportunity to do this again. Right now, I want to finish up and head home."

My cell phone vibrated and chirped to indicate there was a text message. I picked up the phone while Daniel was still trying to persuade me to go to the lounge. It was Lawrence asking what time we could meet.

I repeated myself by saying, "I'll take a rain check." "Hey Daniel, I'll get back to you. My time is up here and I'm going to pack it up and spend some time with my man. I just don't feel like hanging out tonight. You understand...right?"

"Yeah, I do. I'm just trying to cheer you up. I owe you! Thanks again."

I organized the folders and the papers before I left work. I walked out of my office to get in the elevator. I began texting Lawrence after pressing the L button to go to the lobby.

Kim: I'm on the way babe...where are you?

Lawrence: I'm at the store picking up some food for us. I'll cook for you tonight!

Kim: Thanks! I need that type of attention after all that I've been through recently.

The elevator doors opened.  I walked through the elegant lobby that had marble floors and tall glass windows in all directions.  The sliding glass doors that led to the parking garage opened.  I pulled out the keys to my BMW 528i and unlocked the doors.  I sat down, started the engine, and got another text from Lawrence.

Lawrence: Can't wait to see you.

Kim: Same here.  I'll see you there.  Do you want me to get anything?

Lawrence: No, I got everything.

Kim: I bet you do.  I like your style.  See you soon.  Driving home now.

The conversation we had gave me my second wind.  I was excited for once.  A perfect time to let my hair down and live a little.

Reaching for the CD case, I found a Jill Scott CD and slid it into the CD player. Backing out of my parking spot, I started thinking, time to get my evening started.

On the way to the house, I turned on the air conditioning and turned up the music.

When I got to my three-level luxury townhouse in the suburbs, I got more excited because Lawrence was already there. I pressed the button to open the garage. After gracefully parking my car in the garage, I grabbed my stuff and strolled into the house. I walked up to the second level where the kitchen was. Lawrence had not been there long. He was still unpacking the groceries while wearing his Bull's basketball jersey and some black sweatpants.

"Hey babe!"

I had a seductive smile on my face to let him know that I was in the mood for anything. Soon after I put my purse and bag by the kitchen island, I went up behind Lawrence and gave him a tight hug from behind.

With a low smooth voice, he uttered, "I missed you too!"

Lawrence turned around to kiss my lips and I began to rub the crotch of his sweatpants. We kept kissing and I kept rubbing until he was aroused and protruding from his sweatpants.

He said, "I see what you are in the mood for."

He used his foot to slide the grocery bags out of her way.  With the extra room, I got freaky really quick.  We stopped kissing so I could unbutton my blouse and he pushed his sweatpants to his ankles.  I put my hand on his erection and started rubbing it.

"I couldn't wait to get home to be with you. I just need to get my mind off of things for a while.  Help me relax babe."

I reached down to take off my heels with one hand. Our eyes were locked in on each other the whole time.  I started pulling and stroking his erection in every direction with my other hand.

After that, I put both hands on his thighs and slid down until I was eye level with his crouch.

He said, "I love you babe!"

He watched me open my mouth wide enough to give him oral pleasure.  I pleased him with my warm mouth for a short while and then I stood up to kiss him some more.  He then turned me around to help me get undressed.

I bent over right there at the island in the middle of the kitchen. He made me spread my legs as he slid his erection into my wetness.

I moaned as he was moving in and out of me. His strokes became faster and faster. Our skin was slapping together like a stripper making her ass clap at a strip club. He grabbed my shoulders with two hands and put every inch of him in me until I gasped. I took a deep breath and started moaning louder and said, "Give it to me babe! Give it to me!" His stroke got deeper and faster until I climaxed. The secretion flowed down my legs, which could be seen on the dark brown hardwood floor. He kept the same pace until he pulled out and ejaculated all over me.

He hobbled over to the counter on the right like a duck because his sweatpants were around his ankles. He pulled a few sheets of paper towels while I laughed at the way he was walking back to me. I didn't move.

I was in the same position when Lawrence took the paper towels and wiped the semen off my backside. He used the remainder of the paper towels to wipe the floor clean.

He said, "I'll mop the floor tomorrow."

I stood up and said, "Whew...that was good!"

"Yeah, you know how I put it down."

"Yes, I do.  That's why I love you."

"Let me hear you say it again."  He was so happy to hear me say that.

"Okay.  I love you."

Lawrence pulled up his sweatpants.  He had a smirk on his face like...yeah, I'm the man! There was an awkward silence while he got himself together and washed his hands.

I walked over to the couch and turned on the TV.

I asked, "Do you truly love me?"

Lawrence paused and thought for a minute.

"You know what?  I can honestly say that I do love you.  We have been together for a while."

"Yeah, seventeen months.  You've been by my side through it all.  That is why I love you, Lawrence.  Plus, the sex is excellent!"

"I love you too. You're my type of lady and I'm here to stay."

I looked in his direction. "Good! I can help you cook."

"Relax, I'll take care of you tonight Kim."

"Okay...okay, I'm going to take a shower. I'll come back downstairs to lay on the couch while you pamper me tonight."

Lawrence finished taking the food out of the bags. "Yes, that's what you should do! I'll be down here waiting for you."

I grabbed my purse and clothes before I went upstairs. Lawrence began to cook and clean as he prepared a home cooked meal for me. In the bedroom, I took off my bra and put my clothes by the hamper. Walking around naked, I stopped at the mirror to take a look at myself. I ran my fingers through my hair and turned sideways to look at my physique. I went to the dresser to get a ponytail holder.

When I turned around, Lawrence was standing outside the room with two cold glasses of wine. He stood and watched me walk toward him.

"Damn! You look good!" He walked closer to hand me the glass of wine.

"Let's toast!"

We met in the middle of the bedroom. We took the glasses and made them gently collide to make the clink sound that wine glasses make.

Lawrence said, "To us and our newfound love!"

I smiled, "To us!"

The phone rang. I walked over to the small table, where my purse was, to answer it. Lawrence went into the bathroom, turned on the bath water, added the bubbles, and used his cell phone to stream some slow R&B music.

My mood was destroyed while I was on the phone talking to my aunt. My aunt Karyn called to check on me and to find out about the case. I quickly answered her questions and got off the phone. I was in love and had not thought about Morgan and the search for at least an hour or so.

When Lawrence came out of the bathroom, he saw the look on my face.

"What's wrong?"

I knew I looked depressed, which indicated
that my bliss was gone.

I walked to the bathroom where Lawrence was.
"My aunt called to check on me.  She asked
about Morgan.  I told her no new news yet."

He sat down next to me, and I put my head on
his shoulder.

Lawrence looked in my eyes, "We'll get back
to that in the morning.  For now, let's enjoy
the moment.  I know you have cried many tears
and your days of sorrow have been far too
many.  I'm home now!  I'll help you get
through this.  Go take a quick shower, then
relax in the tub.  I'll be back.  I have to
check the food."

I smiled and kissed him.  "Okay.  Can you
bring me another glass of wine?"

"Sure, I'll bring it up after I check the
food."  Lawrence walked out of the room, then
headed to the kitchen.

I put my hair in a ponytail, covered my hair
with a shower cap, and took a quick shower.
I stepped out of the shower slowly and walked
over to check the tub water to make sure it
wasn't too hot.  It was very warm but not too
hot.  I turned off the water,

then got in the oversized freestanding tub
that I had installed to add a dramatic look
to my custom styled bathroom.

My favorite Anita Baker song started
streaming from the phone as I grabbed another
towel and folded it. I got in the tub, took
off my shower cap and put the towel at one
end of the tub so I could rest my head.

I felt relaxed while I was laying back in the
tub, but the fear of bad news about Morgan
was looming in my mind.

Lawrence returned with the bottle of wine. I
carefully grabbed my glass of wine that was
on a little table near the tub and drank it
quickly. I handed it to Lawrence so he could
refill it. He filled it up. This time, I
drank half the glass before he left the
bathroom.

"Damn babe! Take it easy. Getting drunk
like this won't make the problem go away.
The problem will still be here in the
morning."

I looked at him eye to eye. "Yeah, I know
Lawrence. Right now, I want to get faded. I
don't want to think about my situation right
now."

"I got it.  Here, I'll leave the bottle with you.  He stood up and looked at me with compassion.  I'll be done cooking in about 40 minutes.  I'll open another bottle of wine. Once we're done, I'll take advantage of you!"

I smirked, "I'm all yours tonight and forever."

"That's right," Lawrence replied.

He turned off some of the lights in the bathroom and said, "I'll be back."

I drank two more glasses of wine while he was downstairs.  The bottle was empty.  I laid back and closed my eyes while the music put me in a calm mood.  Lawrence was downstairs making chicken Marsala, crescent rolls, Cesar salad and he bought a carrot cake from the store for dessert to eat after the meal.

I was in the tub dozing off.  After Lawrence checked the food, he went upstairs to the guest bedroom to take a shower.  He didn't want to disturb me while I was trying to relax.  He washed up quickly, went to the master bedroom and got some clean clothes out of his luggage.  He started thinking, I spend so much time over here, maybe I should move in with her.  He decided to save the conversation for dinner.

He put on some silk pajamas and sprayed on some cool water cologne.

The timer on the oven was beeping. He ran downstairs to check the food for the last time. The crescent rolls were done. The chicken Marsala was cooked to perfection. Lawrence used a fork to see how tender it was. He flipped the chicken over and turned off the burner on the stove. He put the cover on the pan, grabbed some plates and set the dining room table. The dining room had dark wood floors and a dark colored table to match. It was well decorated with six different sized candles and three nice paintings on the dining room walls.

He tossed the salad and put the Cesar dressing and the salad bowl on the table. He pulled out the plates and shiny utensils. Lawrence grabbed the crescent rolls and placed them on their plates along with the chicken Marsala. After that, he garnished the plates with some fresh parsley and put everything on the table, including two glasses of water. He lit the candles and had everything set for a romantic dinner.

Lawrence came upstairs to get me out of the tub. When he got to the bathroom, he turned on the lights and realized that I was sleeping in the tub. He bent down and gently kissed me.

"Oh, you scared me," I said in a silent sleepy voice.

"That wine knocked you out! Come on, let's get you dried off."

Lawrence held his hand out and pulled me out of the tub. My hands and feet were wrinkled. He grabbed my towel, dried me off and walked me to the bed. Instantly, I was looking around as if I was searching for something that I couldn't see.

"What's wrong, babe?"

"I had a dream about my sister. You know what? It was more like a vision."

"Really! What did you see?"

I took the towel, dried my back a little more, then I sat there on the bed with the towel on my shoulders trying to remember everything I saw.

"When I had the vision, I saw my sister in a room. The room was gray. There was some type of machine with three doors in another room. We were trying to talk to each other, but I couldn't hear what she was saying."

Sitting there naked and confused, I took the towel off my shoulders and closed my eyes.

Lawrence sat on the bed right next to me and wrapped his arm around my shoulder to console me. His warm body next to mine felt comforting. We sat there in silence. The aroma of a home cooked meal was in the air, but I had no appetite.

"Are you okay?" Kissing my shoulder and moving down my arm.

"You smell so fresh and feminine."

I was blushing. "Thank you! It's just juices and berries."

We both laughed at that joke.

"I'll be okay. It's just nerve-racking. My emotions are all over the place. I want to cry but what good would that do. I'm mad and scared, but you being here is helping a lot."

"That's what I'm here for. Whatever you need, I'm right here."

He caressed my naked body. I closed my eyes again. "You make me feel so warm inside. I feel protected."

I heard my cell phone ringing. It was near my purse on the other side of the bedroom. I stood up. I didn't feel like talking, but I did wonder who it was.

Lawrence said, "I'll get your phone."

I grabbed the lotion off the nightstand and moisturized my body. He came back to the bed with my phone and my purse.

While reaching his hand in my purse, he said, "I hope I don't pull out anything that I'm not supposed to see."

"What do you mean?"

He handed me the cell phone and continued to look through my purse.

"I hope I don't find any condoms, phone numbers, hotel card keys...you know what I'm talking about."

"Lawrence, please!" I said with a straight face. "I threw all that stuff away when you told me you were in town."

He gave me a stern look like he wanted to slap me. But I started laughing because he didn't know if I was playing or not. He started laughing and dropped my purse on the floor.

"Yeah, you better be playing!"

"You know I'm kidding. I haven't had random sex with anyone. I had lunch with a

colleague but that's about it. I've been
here saving myself for you."

"Well, once I win this contract, I won't have
to travel as much. I can hire more employees
and lease office space close by. We can buy
a house."

"Hold up Lawrence. I love you, but we have
to plan things out. It will take time to
sell my townhouse. You're renting, so it is
easy for you to close shop and move to a new
place. Besides, we're not married. I'm not
buying a house unless we're married, or we
have a kid on the way."

I had my phone in my hand. I looked down at
the phone to check the missed call.

I didn't recognize the number, but I heard
the chime from the phone that indicated a
voicemail was created.

"Lawrence, let's go downstairs so we can eat.
But first, let me put on some clothes."

I put on my blue comfortable pajama set which
consisted of boy shorts and a matching shirt.
Then I grabbed my cell phone and followed his
lead downstairs. When we got downstairs,
Lawrence pulled out my chair so I could sit.
I sat down and he dropped down to one knee.

I was shocked and pleasantly surprised. He grabbed my hand and smiled. "I thought about you every day. I realized that I love you and now I know that you love me too. I want to make this official. I can move out of my place when my lease ends. I can move in with you until we get married. How does that sound?"

I started tearing up.

"I didn't know that you loved me as much as I love you until today, Kim. Are you sure you love me?"

"Yes, I'm sure Lawrence! We can talk about you moving in, but let's slow down! I thought you were asking me to marry you!"

"Nah, I'm just practicing!"

"Boy, you play too much!"

My exciting evening got interrupted when my cell phone rang again. I picked up the phone and noticed the unfamiliar number again. This time I answered it with tears of joy on my face.

"Hello."

"Hi, is this Kim?"

The sound of an elderly lady made me think of Mabel.

"Yes, is this Mabel?"

"Yes! You remember me. I've been known to forget a person's name 10 minutes after meeting them."

We chuckled a little.

"Is everything okay Mabel? Did you get some info about Gene and why they were down there?"

"No, but the police are here searching for something. Kim, my husband is a mortician that owns a funeral home. Child, they're asking all types of questions. I thought you should know."

"That's good! The police are still hot on the case. I wish I could come down there, but by the time I get there, they'll be gone. I'll call the cop that I know to find out what's going on."

I was stunned and got quiet on the phone.

"Are you doing okay Kim?"

"Yes. Well, I'm trying to stay positive."

"Keep holding on.  Okay, keep holding on.
God will see you through this."

"I agree.  I'm a firm believer.  Well, thanks
for calling.  I'll save your number
and let you know what's going on with the
investigation when I get some info."

"Okay Kim.  Have a good one!"

"What's going on?"  Lawrence asked.

"There was an older lady at the hospital when
I went there to see if Daymon was still
alive.  She's Gene's aunt.  She helped raise
him when his mother was working two jobs.
Anyway, she was telling me that the police
are down there asking questions, you know...
interrogating people."

I stopped talking to take a few bites of my
food.

"Mabel, the lady I was on the phone with, has
a husband running a business.  Guess what it
is?"

"I don't know," Lawrence retorted, "A soul
food restaurant?"

"Nope, he owns a funeral home.  Her husband
is a mortician, Lawrence."

They were both eating at that time. After I made my statement, I paused and thought about the worst.

I finished chewing the food that was in my mouth, sat back, and gazed at the ceiling.

Lawrence uttered, "Are you thinking what I'm thinking? They could've buried Morgan out there real easy."

I had the look of fear on my face as I froze and looked at the cell phone. A million and one bad thoughts were passing through my mind. I thought about calling Frank to get some information. At that point, I was ready to go down south to do some investigating myself.

I picked up the phone and called Frank instead. I let the phone ring until I was able to leave a voicemail.

I left a message and ended the call. Lawrence and I ate in silence as I nibbled on my food and continued to think about the funeral home.

Lawrence could not take the awkward silence anymore and started asking questions.

"What are you thinking about Kim?"

He looked curiously into my eyes, took the last bite of his meal, and placed the fork on the plate.

"The funeral home," I replied.

I picked up the cell phone and called Mabel back. The phone rang once and then Mabel answered.

"Hello."

"Mabel. This is Kim."

"I know darling. What's going on?"

"I didn't talk to the cop that I know yet."

I got up from the table, walked around the dining room, and the kitchen. Leaving my food to get cold.

"Why didn't you tell me about the funeral home? That's vital information." I said in a serious tone.

"Child, I'm sorry. I'm 78. At this age, things slip my mind. I'm not quick on my toes like I used to be. I didn't think anything of it because Gene and Daymon were down here for only a few hours."

"Gene told me that he had a friend who was interested in the funeral business. He set up an arrangement with my husband to talk about starting a new funeral home. Child, I stayed out of it and let the men talk on the phone. You know what I mean...right?"

"Yeah...I do," I answered.

"I need to come down there. I want to take a look around. There's a reason they came down there. Think about it, Mabel. My sister comes up missing and all of a sudden, they decide to visit a funeral home. Daymon is in the fashion business. He doesn't know about the after world and embalming a body. What did Gene do for a living?"

"Well, let me think. He was a hair stylist. He was working on getting his own salon," Mabel responded.

"See! It doesn't add up. My sister is down there. I'm coming down there within a day or so. I'm going to keep calling Frank until he returns my call. I'll call you back," I started reacting with a sense of urgency.

I quickly said bye and ended the call. I didn't give Mabel time to say goodbye. I was pacing through the dining room and the kitchen. Lawrence watched the whole thing unfold and inquired about the trip that I spoke of.

Lawrence asked, "So, we're going somewhere? A funeral home?"

"Yeah babe! We're going down south."

"Where down south?"

"Petersburg, VA."

I stopped pacing and went close to Lawrence to get a hug. I placed my head on his chest and wrapped my arms around him. We stood there embracing each other for a moment. Then, I grabbed his hand and led him to the island in the kitchen to sit him down. The boy shorts and tight V-neck shirt showed my curves and smooth legs.

Lawrence sat on the counter stool, staring intently at my cleavage while I walked around the kitchen island. I made it seem like a courtroom in the kitchen. Lawrence was the jury, and I was the lawyer. I stated all the facts, one by one.

"So, Morgan goes to NJ to see Daymon. She disappears. Gene's place goes up in flames with him still inside. He dies, and now we know that prior to all this, Gene and Daymon went to Petersburg to visit a funeral home."

Lawrence was giving me his undivided attention when he interjected, "They were definitely up to something. What were they doing down there?"

"You don't get it!" I exclaimed. "They took my sister down there! My sister is down there!"

I dropped to my knees and started crying and praying at the same time. With my hands together in prayer position I began to say, "Please don't let my sister be dead." I said that repeatedly.

Lawrence was wearing sweatpants and a tank top showing his masculine build. He sat on the hardwood floor and consoled me.

"Whenever you want to go, we can go. Call that guy Frank and find out what's going on. I'm ready to go right now if you want to. It's about two hours from here. Call the lady back and get the address."

Lawrence took control of the situation and started calling the shots.

I handed Lawrence the phone with tears in my eyes. I was not quite ready to talk. Lawrence looked at the screen on the phone and said, "Is it the 804 number? What is the lady's name...Mabel?"

I shook my head and quietly said yes. He
stood up and found a pen and paper. He
dialed the number, gave Mabel a brief
introduction, then asked her for the address
of the funeral home in Petersburg, VA. Mabel
obliged and gave him whatever he asked for.

Mabel asked, "How is Kim holding up?"

"She's in a state of shock right now. She's
been crying a lot."

"Oh no! Call me when y'all get down here.
My husband and I will meet you and Kim and
take y'all wherever y'all need to go."

There was another call coming in. Someone
else was trying to reach me.

Lawrence quickly said, "Thank you. I wrote
down all the info. There's someone on the
other line."

"Okay...bye," Mabel replied.

Lawrence clicked over. "Hello," he bellowed.

"Can I speak to Kim?" A female voice
requested.

"She can't talk right now. Who is this?"

"Tammy! Who is this?"

"Lawrence."

"Oh yeah, I remember you. Is she okay? Did they find her sister?"

"Not yet. She is emotional right now. I will tell her that you called."

"Take care of her. That's my girl. I would be over there right now, but I have some drama on my side of town too. Let her know I called."

"Okay, I will."

Lawrence walked back over to where I was. I was still on the floor with a serious, but worried look on my face. He reached down to lift me up. I stared in his eyes and followed his lead to the couch in the living room.

He pleaded, "Lay down on the couch with me. But first, let me close the curtains. It's dark as hell outside."

"I don't want them closed Lawrence."

"Listen! I got you, okay! You have to let me take care of you. I won't close all the curtains. How about that?"

"Thank you."

He took a few minutes to close some of the curtains. When he came back to the living room he asked, "So, what's the plan?"

I looked at him with a blank stare.

"So, you want to go down to Petersburg in the morning?"

I nodded yes.

"Okay. By the way, Tammy called."

I sat up in disbelief. "What did she say?"

"She asked how you were doing and told me to tell you to call her."

I relaxed and laid my head on one of the pillows that was on the couch.

# CHAPTER 4

## STEVE

Earlier that night, Steve ran into Calvin at the grocery store. Calvin didn't recognize Steve because he was sporting a hoodie with a dark blue fitted cap that was pulled down near his eyebrows. Steve was ready to fight as his anger started to take over his emotions. He realized that he was at the store and didn't want to cause a scene with the cameras and the many witnesses that were there shopping at the store. Steve was staying with his cousin Omega who was outside taking a nap in a black and gray Ford F250 with tinted windows. Steve was buying some food to cook on the grill. He grabbed his last item, which was the steak sauce, and quickly headed to the register. He decided to go through the self-checkout to speed up the process. Calvin was nowhere in sight. Steve got to the truck and put the three bags of groceries on the floor behind his seat. He then got in and sat there quietly for a few seconds. Omega was stretching and yawning like a bear waking up after hibernating. He looked over at Steve.

"What's wrong with you?"

Steve had a look on his face like he was really concentrating on something. He snapped out of his concentration mode and said, "I saw someone I need to get at."

Omega saw the vindictive expression that Steve had on his face. Steve looked at the door mirror and saw Calvin walking to his car. Steve pointed to the ignition and told Omega to start the engine.

"What's up man! You're acting like you're on a mission."

Steve replied, "Yep, just hold on for a few minutes." Steve was still looking at the door mirror, then he looked through the back window.

"You see that dude? That's the nigga that's fucking Tammy?"

Omega looked puzzled, "Yeah, I can't see his face that good. He's too far away?"

Calvin drove by in his late model red BMW.

Steve pointed at the BMW as it passed by the truck, "Let's follow him."

Omega got excited, "Oh shit! Yeah, let's get up with that nigga."

Omega was a well-built brown skin guy who was
rowdy. The type of guy you want with you if
a fight breaks out at a club. They followed
Calvin to the gas station while the sun was
setting. They parked the truck far from the
gas pumps. Calvin wasn't prepared for what
was going to happen next.

Omega questioned. "What's the plan cousin?
You tryin' to get him right now?"

Steve with a watchful eye said, "Nah, not
here. Let's see where he's going from here.
You got the burner with you?"

"Nah, not in this joint. I got the stun gun
up in here."

Omega reached in the arm rest and pulled it
out. He pressed the button to make the blue
electric spark visible between the two metal
prongs.

Steve was satisfied when Omega passed it to
him, "Yeah, that's all we need. I'm not
gonna kill him, but he's gonna get fucked up
tonight! Let's see where he's going."

Omega put the truck in gear and followed
Calvin for 15 minutes until they arrived in
Calvin's neighborhood. To ensure they would
not be seen, Omega parked the truck four

houses away from Calvin's house. Steve took his cap, hoodie, and tee shirt off.

He put the hoodie back on and wrapped the tee shirt around his face like a bandanna. Then, he pulled the hood onto his head. The only thing that was visible was his eyes.

Omega pulled out his black motorcycle helmet and gloves that were on the floor behind his seat. He got out of the truck and went behind the seat to grab some work gloves. He passed them to Steve.

Omega said, "Let's rush him when he opens the front door."

Steve didn't say a word. He just gave Omega a pound with his fist. Steve and Omega were partners in crime back in the day. They were all too familiar with mischief behavior.

Calvin was checking his voicemail messages. When he was done, he put his cell phone in his pocket and began to get the bags out of his car. With his keys and one bag in his right hand, Calvin grabbed five more bags with his left hand. When he started walking to the front door, it was difficult for him to keep his balance because he had so many groceries bags on his left side. When he reached the front door, he opened the screen door and let it rest on his shoulder as he unlocked the door.

Calvin went into the house, turned on the lights, and turned off the security system. Omega and Steve moved swiftly and got closer to Calvin's house.

Steve said, "I'm going to the bushes. When he goes back inside with more bags, we get him." Omega nodded his head and kneeled down by Calvin's neighbor's car. Steve kneeled down by the bushes.

The streetlight near Calvin's house was not working, which helped cover the two attackers in darkness. Omega saw Calvin turn on the porch lights to illuminate the driveway and walkway. He came outside to get more bags. Unaware of the impending event, Calvin opened the trunk to grab six more bags, then he closed the trunk and the car door. His hands were full with three bags of groceries in each hand. He was not equipped to defend himself. Calvin walked to the door doing arm curls with the bags that he had in his hands. He heard someone running toward him when he opened the screen door. By the time he turned around to see where the footsteps were coming from, it was too late. They caught him by surprise. Steve got to him first.

"What the fuck!" Calvin shouted.

Steve wrapped his left arm around Calvin's neck. With the stun gun in his right hand, Steve proceeded to shock him by putting the stun gun on the skin of his arm until Calvin fell to the floor yelling at the top of his lungs. Omega quickly followed and closed the front door.

After forcing their way into the house, Calvin turned his body around and was now facing his attackers. He started to plea with them, "Please stop man! I'll give you whatever you want!"

During the tussle, the groceries were scattered all over the floor. Calvin was in pain. He was squinting, trying to get a good look at the man with the helmet. Omega started to kick and stomp Calvin from his legs to his ribs. When Omega was done, Calvin was curled up in the fetal position.

Steve stood over Calvin and put the stun gun to the back of his neck. This time he held the button for almost a minute. The second shock left Calvin subdued, causing excruciating pain and muscle contractions. Steve stepped over Calvin and kicked him in the face and stomped on his head twice causing his mouth and nose to bleed.

Calvin's bloody face was all Steve wanted to
see.

"You good!" Omega shouted.

Omega bent down, reached into Calvin's back
pocket, and took his wallet. Steve kicked
Calvin in the back. Omega noticed that
Calvin wasn't moving. Omega motioned with
his hand and said, "Come on!"

Omega turned off the lights and opened the
door. Steve pulled the shirt down from his
face and peeked outside to see if anyone was
out there.

Steve looked left and right, "We're good!
Come on!"

They both jogged to the truck. They jumped
in, started the engine, and looked at each
other. Omega took his helmet off.

They were both sweating profusely.

Steve looked around to see if any neighbors
had come outside. He saw headlights and told
Omega, "Hold on, somebody coming."

The car drove by, stopped at the stop sign,
then kept on going. Omega put the truck in
gear and sped off.

He made the tires squeal when he made the right turn at the stop sign.

Steve frowned at Omega and asked, "Why in the hell did you take his wallet?"

Omega slowed down and started steering the truck with his knee while taking off his gloves. Omega replied, "To make it look like a robbery."

Steve's confusion was gone. He was satisfied with his cousin's answer and began to laugh. Omega gave Steve a fist bump and put his hands back on the steering wheel.

"I got you cousin! Besides, that nigga deserved it."

They both started laughing after realizing that they had just got away with yet another caper.

# CHAPTER 5

## KIM

I awoke when I heard my cell phone ringing again.  I was glad to wake up without a dream about my sister.  The nap was well needed after my meal and all the wine I consumed.

My attention was drawn to the sound of the ringing cell phone on the kitchen counter. The phone stopped ringing before I was able to answer the call.  I picked up the phone and stared at the screen.  A missed call from Frank is what I saw.  I immediately called him back.  The battery was low, so I looked for a spare charger in one of the kitchen drawers.  I connected the phone to the charger and leaned against the wall.

"Hello Kim, I see I missed your call.  We're wrapping up down here.  There are a few employees that did not show up to work today. We are going to stay down here over night and talk to the rest of the staff in the morning."

"Good!  Frank, I want to come down there.  I know my sister is down there.  Think about it.  Why would they travel four or five hours to go to a funeral home?  Then, Gene's condo explodes."

"When I spotted Daymon in his part of town, he tried to get away from me when he noticed that I was following him. He started driving too damn fast and ended up in the hospital because he crashed trying to avoid me."

"You sure do state the facts just like a lawyer. I know that you're good at what you do. Your dad was proud of you. I hear you Kim, it sounds like they came down here to do something other than get a tour of a funeral home."

"You're right! I have never heard my sister nor Daymon ever talk about starting a business, let alone a funeral home."

"So far, we haven't found her. No one has seen your sister, and no unidentified bodies were found. The funeral home has a security system with cameras, but the system is old. The nighttime footage is garbage. I told the owner to upgrade the cameras. It has been 3 weeks Kim. No witnesses and no evidence." Frank looked disappointed.

"All we have is the half ass confession from the video that was on the cell phone that Gene had. He basically said he did something bad but gave no particular details.

Everything is pointing to Daymon. We know he can't talk. We're running out of options."

"That's the last thing I want to hear Frank."

"I know. Well, I 'll see you tomorrow if you're still coming down here. If anything comes up, I'll call you."

"Okay."

We ended the call, and Frank went back to talking to the other cops that were from that area.

I went upstairs to gather my things for the morning trip.

## CHAPTER 6

### TAMMY

Throughout this ordeal, Tammy was at her single family beach house with her girls getting tipsy while talking about the situation between her and her husband. The beautifully decorated four story house was lavish. It had three spacious front porches, six bedrooms, and five bathrooms. The ground floor is where the garage was located. The first floor had an open floor plan with a modern kitchen, large dining area, and a cozy living room with a flat screen TV, surround sound, gas fireplace, and a half bathroom. On the second floor, there were three bedrooms with two full bathrooms. Lastly, the third floor master suite had a unique tray ceiling, walk in closet, and a spa like master bathroom. There was also a seating area on that floor with a back balcony, and two extraordinary bedrooms with a shared bathroom.

Leslie and Mary were at the house with Tammy. Mary, Tammy, Kim and Leslie have been friends since their college days. Mary was Tammy's roommate from the University of Maryland Eastern Shore. They were making Mojitos and tossing them back like pros.

They laughed, talked, and listened to music as they cooked a meal and sipped their drinks. Tammy bought the food, Leslie brought the alcohol, Mary helped cook as she cracked jokes and had them all laughing. Mary was the comedian of the group. She had a lot of connections and always knew people wherever she went. They were making Chicken Alfredo, spinach, and corn on the cob with garlic bread. Knowing and hanging out with Mary meant getting into all types of parties for free most of the time. Tonight was no different. One of Mary's social media connections informed her about a party at a beach house that was not too far from where they were staying in Ocean City. Mary was texting and taking selfies to update her social media page. The night was planned. Tammy was venting and acting like she did nothing wrong, and her husband was overreacting.

Leslie said, "You know what? Steve should trust Tam, but how would you feel if Steve was hanging out with another woman."

"He ain't going nowhere!"

"What if he did Tam? Would you ask him questions? Would you believe his story?"

"I don't know.  But he should know better than to accuse me of some shit!"

Mary said, "You two will work through it. But, for now, you have to lay in the bed that you made."

Tammy said, "What are you talking about?"

"Revenge!  If my husband did that to me, I would make him think I was dating multiple men.  I'd get dressed up and go out wearing something sexy and look at him like, what? He would be calling me trying to find out where I'm at and who I'm with.  Steve could be at the strip club right now trying to get back at you.  You know what goes on in the VIP?  Some of those girls would do anything for money."

"Yeah, I hear ya.  Who knows where that nigga is right now.  He's not answering my calls."

"You pissed him off!  You gonna have to do the nasty big time if you want to make up with him," Mary mentioned.  "I did it when I was dating tall Greg.  I would give him the best head to resolve any argument that I caused."

"How that work out for ya?  He ain't around anymore," Tammy jokingly interrupted.

"He wouldn't hold up his end consistently. He wouldn't help me with the rent, but he was always at my place eating my food and my pussy. He was good for multiple organisms, but it seemed like he was using me. I was holding him down while he was serving me good dick. I came to my senses. He wasn't bringing much to the table, and he would make some dumb decisions sometimes. So, I let him go. He couldn't help me grow. He was just good at making me cum again and again. Believe me Tammy. You got a good man at home. He's funny, he goes to church, he has his own money, and he knows how to throw a good party. What else do you want?"

Feeling real tipsy from the drinks they were serving up. Tammy blurted out, "He has good credit too!"

They all laughed.

Mary got serious. "Listen y'all. These guys out here are married with kids, or they're not trying to settle down in a monogamist relationship. They're immature, they're quick draw McGraw in the bed, and the list goes on."

Leslie chimed in, "You ain't never lied girl! I dated a guy like that. He was from Virginia. Nice job, nice house, and he had his stuff together. But he never made me cum. I would tell him what to do, but he could never get the job done...know what I mean?"

They all nodded their heads.

Leslie said, "Let's go! Let's see if any good prospects are out here."

Mary and Tammy agreed. They finished their drinks and got themselves together. Mary turned up the music that was coming from the portable wireless speaker that she brought with her. They all took a shower, put on makeup, and came out of their rooms looking photo shoot ready. Tammy was the shortest in the group. She had on skintight black Bebe jeans with a white silk shirt and her Louis Vuitton sneaker boots that went well with her beautiful dark skin tone. Mary was brown skin with dreads, and she stood a little taller than Tammy with her blue jeans, Burberry shirt and tan heels.

Leslie was the tallest and slimmer than her girls. Her light skin complexion was flawless. Her black heels and her brown and black jump suit insinuated her butt perfectly. They all met back in the kitchen for another drink before they hit the road.

"I hope this place we're going to is nice," Tammy uttered.

Mary finished making the drinks and passed a cup to Leslie and the other cup to Tammy.

"This is our night to turn up!" Tammy said.

"Yeah! I can have a good time anywhere. We can crack jokes on everybody. You know how we do it Tam." Mary replied.

Mary took out her phone and sent a text.

"Let me get the address to find out exactly where the party is."

They sipped on their Mojitos. Then, Leslie bust out in laughter.

"Hey, remember that time we were at the airport going to Cancun? We were talking about everyone that walked by. I was laughing so hard that day. Tears were coming out of my eyes."

Tammy chimed in. "Yeah, remember that guy sat next to Mary with the suit that was way too tight.  He thought Mary was trying to holla at him, but she was trying to find out why he was wearing that tight ass suit.  You made that guy so uncomfortable.  I saw some of the people sitting around us laughing at the things she was saying."

"He had it coming.  I couldn't resist," Mary replied.  She got a text, then she put the address in her GPS app.  She took another sip of her drink, then looked at Tammy.  "It's good to see you smiling again.  The party is seventeen minutes from here."

"She just needed us to remind her of the good times," Leslie added.

"I do feel better.  These drinks are kickin' in too.  I feel so relaxed right now. Thanks for making the trip with me."

Tammy walked over to the counter to get some more pasta to soak up the alcohol.

"Girl you're welcome," said Leslie.

"This place is fly!  You've been talking about this place off and on for a while.  I had to come see what you were talking about. I'm gonna need you to step your game up so we can get butler service and a driver while we're out here.  Just playing girl!  You came

up!  Thanks for not forgetting about us,"
Mary announced.

Mary put her drink down to make a plate.  She
got close to Tammy and gave her a playful
bump with her shoulder.

A smirked spread across Tammy's face as she
looked at both of them.  "We're sisters for
life.  Too bad Kim couldn't make it.  You
three are the only females that have kept it
real with me since day one.  Now we're in our
mid thirties and we're still tight!"

Leslie asked, "What's going on with Kim?  Did
they ever find her sister?"

"No, she's been very busy working with the
police; turning over every stone and looking
into every small detail.  She was resting the
last time I called her.  I spoke to her boo
and he said she's been crying a lot, which is
to be expected.  How selfish of me to try to
get her to come out here to kick it with us
and help me get over my issues with my
husband."

"Damn, I gotta make some time to call her.  I
don't know what to say to her, but she is the
rational one who has been there and done

that. She always has good advice when I call with an issue," Mary proclaimed. "Let's call her on the way to the party. That's our girl! Let's check on her."

Leslie grabbed her cup and raised it in the air. Mary and Tammy did the same with their cups. One. Two. Three! They all took big gulps of their drinks like they were taking shots. They threw the cups into the trash, then Leslie joined them in the feast.

It didn't take long for the ladies to hop in Tammy's white Range Rover and head to the party. They danced to Beyoncé's tune "Drunk in Love," as they let Mary's GPS guide them to the party on shiny 22 inch rims and tan leather seats. They cruised down the street with all the windows down, letting the warm night air flow through the Range Rover. During the drive to the party, they pointed out the best townhouses and beach houses along the way.

They made it to a beach house. All the lights were on, and people were outside kickin' it like it was a block party. Tammy found a parking spot that wasn't too far from the beach house.

They climbed out of the vehicle and gracefully walked over to the crowd that was all around the beach house.  On the inside, it seemed like an old fashion house party.

Good music was playing and there were guys standing around eye bawling every female that walked by.

"What's up love!  Can I get a minute of your time?"

The tall light skin fella said when Tammy, Leslie, and Mary walked through the front door of the beach house.

They all giggled like college girls.  Tammy said, "Come dance with us!  Show us what you're workin' with!"

The other guy that was with the tall light skin fella spoke up.  He was a muscular guy with a brown complexion.  He was the same height as his friend.

"Yeah, we can do that, but it's a little crowded in there, so I hope you don't see nothing wrong with a little bump and grind."

Mary liked his wit.  It was easy to tell that he was in shape by the way his tight polo shirt showed off his biceps.  When they got to the top of the stairs, Mary turned and asked in a playful sarcastic way, "What's your name...R. Kelly?"

"Nah, Mark."

Mary glanced at the other guy from head to toe. "What about you? What's your name?"

"I'm Brian." He said with a cool demeanor.

Mark moved quickly to meet and greet them at the top of the steps. He opened the door. Tammy walked into the house and stood by the front door checking out the party. Leslie was right behind Tammy with a watchful eye on Mary. Leslie was standing in the doorway in a spot where she could see what was going on inside the house where Tammy was, and out in front of the house where Mary was.

There were plenty of people dancing, walking around, or standing somewhere with a drink in their hand. Leslie and Tammy started dancing when the DJ did his mix and faded in the TI and Robin Thicke song "Blurred Lines."

Mary, Brian, and Mark were outside talking by the front door. Mary walked inside once she noticed her girls were having a good time. Mark followed behind her like a little puppy. Brian went to the kitchen. The ladies were

by the front door dancing up a storm.  There
was brown liquor, white liquor, cups and soda
bottles on the table by the kitchen.  The
guys went to the table and poured some drinks
into their cups.

They huddled up and watched the ladies have a
good time while they sipped on their drinks.

Mark started talking to Brian.  "I'm trying
to get at shorty.  Her name is Mary."

"I see you, homie.  You started putting in
work before they got to the front door."

"Yeah, she has a phat ass!  You can see that
shit from the front."

"Hell yeah!  I saw that."

"What about you B?"

"I'm not feeling them.  The other two seem a
little bougie.  But...I'll tag along.  Handle
your business."

The ladies were dancing by themselves in
their own little circle.  They noticed the
guys were staring at them.

Tammy said to Mary, "Girl, he's looking at you like you're his next meal."

"Yep, he's my type, too. Mark might get some if he plays his cards right. He's cute and he has a nice body."

Tammy leaned closer to Mary's ear. "His boy Brian seems like he's up to something. You know they're out here playing the game."

Mary smiled and tried to act naive. "What game?"

"You know, trying to get some pussy for the night."

When Mary saw Brian and Mark approaching, her eyes grew bigger. "Oh shit, here they come."

Mary and Mark start dancing, and Brain followed behind him and started grooving to the music near Tammy and Leslie. They were all having a good time. Brian danced with Leslie and Tammy, but he did not get real close to them. Mark was behind him dancing provocatively with Mary.

Brian noticed the smell of marijuana in the air. When Brian leaned in closer, he asked, "Do y'all smell that?" Leslie and Tammy nodded in agreement.

Leslie was the first to speak up. "Yeah, I smell it. Do you have some?" The aroma of marijuana permeated the four walls of the beach house.

Tammy laughed and walked off to see what else was happening in the beach house, leaving Leslie and Brian alone to mingle. Tammy noticed a good mixture of people. All nationalities were in attendance. She went to the kitchen to find some water. On the way to the kitchen, she saw white girls dancing with each other, black guys dancing with Asian girls, black girls dancing with white guys, Hispanic girls dancing with other Latinos, black guys and white guys standing around. No fights. No drama. Tammy made it to the kitchen and found a lot of picked over food and a bunch of coolers all over the floor. A keg of beer was on the counter in the corner. She looked in the first cooler and found sodas. The second cooler had water bottles. She grabbed three. When she stood up, she was met by a black girl and a white girl that were down for whatever. The black girl tapped Tammy on her ass while Tammy had her back turned.

"Hey, you!"

"Don't do that shit!" Tammy exclaimed.

"I'm sorry. No harm okay," the black female said.

The white female was obviously on some type of drug. The black girl seemed to be high on something, but she was more in control.

"I like those shoes! Those Louis Vuitton shoes and those jeans are showing all your curves. What type of jeans are those?"

"They are called not interested."

"What?" The black female said.

"Maybe you didn't hear me. They're called not interested straight jeans!"

The white female started laughing like she was at a comedy show.

"Listen, thanks for the compliment, but I'm gonna go over there. Don't follow me!"

Tammy walked past the two females and didn't look back. She was ready to go but her friends were having a good time. She felt alone as she thought about her husband who was in Maryland doing his own thing. She felt sorry for what she did, but she didn't show it much.  Tammy was walking past the party people when she heard someone call her name.  It was Mary.  Mary stopped dancing and walked over to Tammy.

"Where ya going?"  Mary asked.

"To the truck to make a call."

It was well past 12am and the party was rocking with no end in sight.

People were inside and outside, drinking and having a great time.  It was a grown and sexy party.  No one was out of control.

"Who you know out here?  Are you trying to make a booty call?"  Mary questioned.

"Nah girl, I'll be right back."  She smiled and gave Mary a water bottle and kept moving forward to the front door.

Tammy made it to her Range Rover.  She hopped in, put the water bottles in the cup holders and took her cell phone out of the arm rest. She sighed and looked at the call list.  She had 3 missed calls, but Steve was not one of them.  She checked her two text messages.

One was from Calvin and the other one was from her sister.

Calvin sent a text early that afternoon asking how things were going after the argument with Steve. He was telling her that he was available to talk if she needed someone to talk to.

Her sister's text read, "Where y'all at? I stopped by but nobody was at the house. Call me."

She checked her social media accounts and saw nothing from Steve. The one person that she wanted to talk to did not bother to contact her while she was gone for an extended weekend. She sat up straight and put her head on the head rest. She made the seat recline slightly and looked at the stars through the sunroof. She opened the sunroof, then rolled down the windows just enough to let the breeze in. She took a deep breath and sighed again.

She pondered. How in the hell am I going to fix this? She called Steve, but he did not answer the phone.

Shortly after thirty minutes had passed, Mary and Leslie came out to check on Tammy. They both noticed Tammy's seat was in the reclined position, as if she was trying to go to sleep. They startled her when they both knocked on the window. Mary and Leslie climbed in the vehicle after Tammy unlocked the doors.

Tammy said, "Y'all scared me! I wasn't expecting anyone to knock on the window."

"Are you okay? Why are you laying back like you're ready to go to sleep?" Leslie asked.

Tammy passed a water bottle to Leslie. Tammy took a drink from the other water bottle that was in the cup holder. She then said, "I'm not excited about this party."

Mary said, "What have you been doing out here? You said you were going to make a call. Who did you call Steve or Calvin?"

Leslie started laughing. "Yeah, we all in your business! So, spill it!"

"I called Steve but he ain't around. Who knows what he's doing right now. He hasn't returned my calls, and he doesn't pick up when I call him."

"Yeah, you kinda fucked up when you made that move with Calvin." Mary proclaimed.

Leslie said, "Roll up the windows."

Tammy started the engine, turned the air
condition on, and pressed the buttons on the
door to make the tinted windows go up.
Leslie showed them the small weed filled
cigar that she had in her possession. She
pulled out a pink lighter from her clutch bag
and lit the small cigar.

Tammy gave Mary and Leslie an evil look, then
a nod. "I don't need that, but y'all can go
ahead and smoke."

Leslie took a long pull and held it in her
lungs, then passed it to Tammy. Leslie blew
the smoke out and looked at Tammy.

"Everyone needs a little weed in their life
from time to time. This will calm you down.
It will be like drinking hot chocolate."

Tammy said, "What the hell! That's right,
we're on vacation!"

Mary said, "That's right...we are!"

Tammy reached her hand out to get the cigar
that had shortened in length, then took a
long pull, and passed it to Mary. Mary took
it and made the smoke come out of her nose
like a pro. Mary passed it to Leslie.

Leslie said, "This is how it was in college. Remember?"

Tammy started coughing and laughing, then Leslie started laughing too. Leslie took another hit and passed it around to the other two, then looked at the two of them and said, "Friends for life!"

Tammy agreed. "Yeah, friends for life!"

Leslie passed it to Mary.

"That's right! Friends for life," Mary said. She inhaled the smoke, held it in her lungs for a few seconds, then put the tiny piece of the weed filled cigar in the water bottle that she had.

Mary closed her eyes and put her head back on the headrest and started giggling.

Tammy looked at Mary, "What girl?"

Leslie chimed in, "Yeah giggles, what's so funny?"

"I got the answer for your problem."

Tammy and Leslie looked at each other and looked back at Mary.

"Oh yeah! Tell me Einstein. How do I get my husband back in my corner?"

Tammy waited patiently for Mary to stop smiling and say what was on her mind.

"Just buy Steve a new car and a Rolex. Then, when you see him, you give him his gifts and give him the best head he has ever had. You better suck his dick really good no matter where you are. Find a secluded place and make him cum. I bet you he'll forgive you then!"

Leslie laughed, "Yep, she has a point!"

Tammy started laughing and shaking her head side to side. She could not believe what Mary was saying.

"The funny thing is, I already thought about that girl!"

They all started laughing.

"So, what's the problem? You got the money to do it," Mary replied.

"Steve is the type of person that will bring it up again and again, then we'll be arguing

like we did before. He had his fist balled
up like he was going to hit me girl. I've
never seen him that mad before. He told me
he doesn't trust me. You can't buy trust.
If I could, I would've ordered it and had it
delivered to the house already!"

Leslie said, "You would've ordered a box of
trust? Girl, I know you're feeling it now.
That weed was pretty good!"

They all had a good laugh after that comment.

"Maybe I should let time heal this situation.
Maybe we should go to marriage counseling.
Then, I'll do what Mary suggested."

They erupted in laughter.

Tammy said, "I'm glad I can laugh about this
situation now."

"I told you; everybody needs a little weed in
their life every now and then."

They all laughed after hearing Leslie's
comment.

Tammy said, "Let's go back inside and get
something to drink. I'm thirsty."

"Yeah, me too."

"Same here."

They all got out of the Range Rover and walked back to the house party.

Tammy gave the empty water bottle that was in the cup holder to Leslie.

"Let's get rid of this."

After a short walk, they made it back to the large beach house. Leslie tossed the bottle in the trash can that was on the side of the house. They went back inside to mingle with the folks at the party. The DJ started playing "Summertime" by Will Smith and DJ Jazzy Jeff. The crowd was into it. Everyone that knew the words to the song was singing along. Tammy, Leslie, and Mary were having a good time with a mellow high. The music was thumping and the three of them were dancing by themselves. Three more songs were played, then Tammy said, "I'm gonna get some more water."

Leslie and Mary went with her. The cooler was in the corner by the kitchen along with the coolers of beer, wine coolers, and sodas.

Empty liquor bottles were on the counter and the food was scarce. Tammy went straight to the cooler that had the water bottles and signaled for the other two to come where she was.  With a glaze of sweat on their faces, they laughed at each other when they noticed how much they were sweating.

Mary yelled over the music, "Girl, that was like a workout!  I felt like I was a choreographer!"

"Yeah, I know!  I'm gonna call you Janet Jackson for the rest of the night because you were dancing like you were in one of her music videos!"

They all laughed hard.

Leslie asked, "How long do y'all want to stay?"

That is when Mark tapped Mary on the shoulder, which left Leslie and Tammy to discuss the plan.

Leslie said, "I'm ready whenever you are." Tammy watched Leslie scan the huge crowd of people as if she was looking for someone.

Tammy asked, "Who you looking for...ol' boy?"

Leslie smiled and gave Tammy a playful push. "I saw him earlier talking to some guy.  They were watching some THOT shake her ass like a stripper. But I'm looking at all the other men in here. It looks like Mary is trying to hook up with Mark tonight. Look at them. He's all in her ear getting his mack on. You know she's a little loose with the booty."

Tammy said, "Nah, nah...she calls it being a free-spirited person."

They both laughed.

They walked toward Mary and Mark.

Mary said to Mark, "Hey, we're about to leave. Let's get some food."

"Y'all hungry? Let's go to IHOP. It's right down the street. My treat," Mark suggested.

"I don't really feel like sitting at the restaurant. Let's get it to go," Tammy explained. "Well, you know y'all can do what y'all want to do. I'm going back to the house."

Brian walked up and put his arm around Mark's shoulders and joined the conversation. He was definitely in a good mood. "What's the deal people! What y'all talking about?"

Mark replied, "They're hungry. I was telling them about the IHOP down the street."

Brian said, "Cheese eggs and Welch's grape. Conversate for a few, cause in a few, we gonna do what we came to do. Ain't that right, boo?"

Leslie said, "True!"

They all laughed. Leslie and Brian were saying the lyrics from one of The Notorious B.I.G songs.

Tammy jumped in the conversation. "I don't feel like going. There's food at the house. I'll meet y'all there."

"Girl, you not coming with us?" Mary asked.

"Nah, I'm good."

"I'll bring you some pancakes."

"Okay! Thanks Les, I'll call you when I get to the house."

Leslie said, "Yeah do that."

Tammy turned around and made her way through the crowd. The rest of them had their attention on Tammy as she walked away. Mary and Leslie knew what was going on with Tammy, so they just looked at each other, shrugged their shoulders, and shook their heads.  Then Brian spoke up.

"What's up with your girl?"

"She's going through it right now...drama at home."

At that time, Tammy made it through the crowd and walked out the front door.

Brian yelled over the music, "I'm ready if y'all are!"

Leslie and Mary started walking and the guys followed.  Not too long after that, they made it to the front door after maneuvering through the mass of people who were dancing, smoking, drinking, or just standing around. The air was crisp, and the sky was full of stars.  Leslie and Mary stood on the steps. They looked around for Tammy's Range Rover. Leslie spotted it.  Tammy was still in the Range Rover with the engine running.

Leslie said, "Oh, she didn't leave yet."

Mary looked at the guys.  "Where did y'all park?"

Brian pulled out the keys and tossed them to Mark.  Mark pressed the button on the key FOB to unlock the doors. The headlights and the signal lights flashed. Brian pointed to the left where a shiny dark blue Audi A8 with shiny rims was parked.

Brian said, "Let's roll out, get some food, and start the after party!"

Mary looked at Mark, "Yeah, we'll see how things go. I hope y'all not taking us to the ghetto IHOP!"

Mark said, "Nah, we got more class than that."

He led the way to the Audi. When they got to the car, Brian opened the back door for the ladies.

"Oh, you're such a gentleman," Leslie mentioned.

Brian looked directly at Leslie. "Thanks! I try to be."

Leslie smiled and slid over to make room for Mary.

Mary chuckled and said, "This is a nice car. Y'all got it smelling like air fresheners and a pound of weed?"

Tammy sent the ladies a group text. "I was waiting to see what car y'all were getting into. I got a picture of the Texas license tag. Be safe." She drove by and beeped the horn.

Mary and Leslie looked at each other and smiled.

Mary texted, "Thanks, we'll text you when we get to IHOP."

Brian got in the car and said, "They're decriminalizing the use and possession of weed all over the place."

Leslie chimed in. "I hear ya, but it's not legal everywhere yet."

"The weed prohibition is almost over." Brian replied.

Mark started the engine, adjusted the seat and the mirrors, then drove off.

"How far is IHOP from here," Mary asked.

"About ten minutes," Mark answered. "What are y'all in the mood for?" Mark questioned.

Leslie said, "A little bit of everything, so I hope you two brought your wallets."

They all started laughing as Mark came to a stop sign. Mark looked in the rearview mirror and said, "I'm ballin' on a budget, so don't get carried away when we get there." Mark and Brian shared a laugh.

Mary said, "What are you waiting for? We've been at this stop sign for a long time. Do you think the stop sign is gonna turn green? Back at the beach house, you said Brian was too messed up to drive. You're in the same boat! You should let me drive." They all laughed.

Mark wanted to show that he was in control. He mashed the gas pedal and made the wheels squeal as he accelerated down the street to take the exit to get onto the highway. They ended up at IHOP in seven minutes flat.

Tammy made it to her beach house. While in the Range Rover, the lights from the dash illuminated the inside of the vehicle. She dialed Steve's number, and it went straight to voicemail. Then she called Steve's mother to see if she had heard from him.

"Hello?"

"Hello mother in-law.  I'm sorry for calling so late.  I haven't been able to reach Steve. Have you heard from him?"

"It's okay...hold on."  Ms. Peterson was in the bed sleeping.  She rolled over, turned on the light, and sat on the edge of the bed.

"First of all, how are doing Tammy?"

Ms. Peterson moved the pillows around and propped herself up in the bed as if she was getting ready for a long conversation.

"I'm not good."

"I spoke to Steve the other day.  He was on my mind, so I gave him a call.  He told me what happened."

Tammy was shocked and embarrassed.  Her palms started to sweat.

"It was a mistake.  I realized I was wrong."

"Tammy, I'm not the one you should be telling this to.  We all make mistakes.  You need to tell Steve all of this.  I was married to Steve's father for 48 years.  I lost count of how many mistakes we made as a married couple.  But we figured out what to do to stay married.

Divorce was never an option. It's hard to find someone that you are compatible with. At my age, I realized what I had when my husband died. Cancer is a slow death sometimes. During that period, when he was going through the Cancer treatment, we apologized for all the things that we did to each other. Nowadays, people get divorced left and right. The point I want to make is, if you want your marriage to last, you should fight for it. You need to constantly work on your marriage to make sure it doesn't go stale. You need to tell Steve what you told me and hope for the best!"

"I'm trying to, but he won't answer the phone when I call."

"Yeah, he is mule-headed like his daddy. Keep trying! Give him a few days to calm down, okay."

"Yes."

"Take care Tammy. I'm going back to sleep."

Tammy got out of the Range Rover and headed up the stairs. She unlocked the door and walked into her empty beach house.

The echo of her footsteps could be heard as she walked across the wood floor on the second level, where the kitchen was located.

She looked around the spacious beach house feeling happy. A slight grin was evident after realizing she could afford the luxurious lifestyle. The grin on her face faded away when she realized she was all alone.

She was still high from the weed they smoked earlier. Tammy put her Chloe Marcie purse on the counter next to the refrigerator. She poured herself a glass of water and drank it quickly. She saw a bag of UTZ potato chips that Mary brought for the road trip. Tammy poured the chips onto a paper towel, then poured herself another glass of the mixed drink that was left over from earlier that evening. She checked her phone. There were no calls from anyone. She walked out to the balcony and raised her head to look at the stars in the sky while putting the chips and the drink on the table. She went back inside to get the Off candle to keep the bugs away. She lit the candle and put it on the table, then sat down to relax.

Sex with Calvin was a thought that crossed her mind. Wishing that they did have sex, she started thinking.

I'm in trouble with my husband and I didn't even let Calvin please me. She thought about the day they hugged after they went out to eat and his hands went lower than they should have. She liked it. She enjoyed the attention that she got from him. While fantasizing about his erection, she knew it was just a matter of time before they would take the plunge and have an affair. Her emotion switched when she thought about Steve having sex with someone else. She was thinking, he might be fucking someone now and that's why he's not answering my calls. That's why we haven't talked in five days.

After guzzling the drink until the glass was empty, she put her elbow on the table and held her head with her left hand while trying to figure out how to get Steve back in her life. She wanted to have her cake and eat it too. A decision needed to be made. Steve was not willing to let Calvin be in her life. Tears came down her face after thinking about losing her husband to another female...the rebound chick.

Her husband was smooth with his words and easy on the eyes. She knew he would have no problems meeting new women.

Her cell phone rang. Tammy was anxious to hear from Steve, but it was Mary calling.

"Hey girl! What are you doing?"

"Sitting outside on the balcony."

"We're on our way back."

"All right. I'm here."

"Okay, we'll be there soon. Bye."

Tammy was feeling sad. A few tears came down her face because Steve was ignoring her calls. She sat out on the balcony with her eyes closed for a few minutes. Before she knew it, 15 minutes went by.

Tammy heard Mary's voice followed by laughter from a man. She wiped the tears from her eyes and went to the kitchen. Leslie knocked on the door. Tammy unlocked the door to let them in. Leslie could tell that Tammy was not happy.

"What's wrong? Are you okay?"

"I'll be okay. You know me!"

Leslie walked in first. Mary followed with Brain and Mark accompanying her.

Brian asked Leslie to stay by the front door so they could talk.

Mary asked, "Is it cool if they eat and hang out a bit?" Mary gave Tammy a wink. Tammy gave a smirk. She did not want to be the party pooper.

Tammy managed to smile, "Yeah, it's cool."

Mark walked in with all the bags. He looked around and said, "Nice place!" He placed the food on the counter and washed his hands in the kitchen sink.

Mary said, "We brought you something. Well, Mark bought you some pancakes and a country omelet."

"Cool, thanks Mark."

Tammy cheered up and gave Mark a genuine smile. She walked over and gave Mark a fist bump while he was taking all the containers of food out of the bags.

"Where's Leslie?" Tammy asked.

"She's outside with Brian," Mary replied.

Mary and Tammy started laughing. Mark was trying to figure out why they were laughing, but he did not bother to ask. Mark pulled out a bag of weed and two cigars. He gutted the cigars, threw the tobacco in one of the bags that the food came in, and started to roll two cigars packed with weed. Tammy walked to the front door to see what Leslie and Brian were doing. That's when Tammy's phone started ringing. She stopped in her tracks and changed direction. Tammy went to the balcony to get her phone that was laying on the table outside. The name on the screen said Jasmine; it was Tammy's sister calling.

"Hello, what's wrong Jas?"

"I got some news about Steve."

Tammy checked the time on her phone. "It's 2 am. What happened Jas?"

Jasmine said, "Hold on."

Tammy looked at Mary with fear in her eyes. She closed the sliding door then took the conversation upstairs. Mary followed Tammy to the master bedroom in the beach house.

Jasmine was taking her earrings off so it would be a little more comfortable holding the phone to her ear.

"Ah, that feels much better.  Tammy?"

"Yeah, I'm still here.  So, what happened?"
Jasmine began to tell the story.

"You remember Dana...right?"

"Yeah, what happened?"  Tammy inquired.

Meanwhile, Mark was alone in the kitchen.
He finished eating, then got up to throw his
container in the trash and wash his hands.

He noticed Tammy's purse on the counter and
stared at it for a few seconds.  He looked
around to see if the coast was clear.

Leslie and Brian were still outside, and
Tammy and Mary were upstairs.  Tammy was
still buzzed off the weed and drinks.  She
forgot all about her black Chloe Marcie
leather purse.  Mark quickly reached into the
purse, grabbed her Gucci wallet, then pulled
out two credit cards and her driver's
license.  Mark took out his phone and quickly
took pictures of the license and the front
and back of the credit cards.  He put them
back the way he found them.  When he heard
the front door open, he put the purse back in
the same spot.  He opened the refrigerator to

act like he was looking for something to drink.

Leslie spoke first, "Where my girls at?  You got them tied up somewhere in this place?" She looked at Mark and Brian and got in her Bruce Lee stance.

They laughed at her.  "Nah, they're upstairs on the phone.  Be easy, we ain't here to hurt you."  Mark replied.

"Yeah, all right!  I was going to use my self-defense skills to take y'all out."  They all laughed.

Brian said, "You would've got fucked up with that karate shit."

He walked over to the counter to get his food.  Leslie started to wonder what was going on upstairs.  She went back into play mode.

"Y'all don't know, but that karate shit works.  I know how to protect myself."

"I bet you do.  I wasn't going to let him hurt you," Brian said.

"You say that now, but who knows.  Let me go upstairs to see what's going on.  They've been up there for a minute." Leslie walked off to go upstairs.

Mark asked, "What's up with her?"

Brian said, "She is a feisty one. She let me rub on her ass and kiss her neck. She might be down. She just plays hard to get. Let's stick around for about two or three hours to see if we can get a happy ending."

Mark said, "True!"

Brian put his food in the microwave and continued to talk to Mark to devise a plan on how they were going to get some pussy that night.

Upstairs, the call was still going on. Leslie walked into the room looking confused. Mary and Tammy were sitting on the bed.

Leslie said, "What's going on? What's up with the secret meeting in the middle of the night?"

Mary got up and walked toward Leslie and started speaking in a low tone, "Something is going on with Steve.   Jasmine found out something!"

Jasmine was on the phone saying, "Dana came to the salon and was telling me how Steve was in the club making it rain.  You know how she's on that bisexual tip...right?"

"Yeah, I know."

"She happened to be at the strip club with her girlfriend and she said Steve was with two other guys and they were tossing money in the air, getting a lot of attention.  She said she lost track of him and the other guy. But one of the guys came out from the VIP room with a big grin on his face.  He was looking around trying to find Steve and the other guy.  He got a lap dance and then he sat at the bar and started texting somebody.  He was talking to the bartender, then within ten minutes or so, he was gone."

Tammy was stunned.  She was quiet for a few seconds.

"Hello...hello," Jasmine shouted.

"I'm still here."

"Are you okay?"  Jasmine questioned.

"Well, we got into a big argument, and I haven't seen Steve in a few days. He's not answering the phone when I call. He's avoiding me."

"What were y'all fighting about?"

"Calvin."

"What about Calvin?"

"Steve thinks we're fucking?"

"Why would he think that?"

"Well, he bought me dinner."

"Calvin, your trainer, brought dinner to your house?" Tammy looked at Leslie and Mary with shame written all over her face.

"No, we were at the new Italian restaurant over by the harbor."

"What the fuck Tammy! That's why Dana was so pressed to tell me that she saw Steve at the strip club. She was saying they were like celebrities in that place. You know how thirsty these young girls are for a nice looking guy with some money. You fucked up!"

"I know.  I know!"

Tammy felt depressed again.  Mary and Leslie saw how distraught Tammy was, so they let her know they were there for her, and they went downstairs to give her a little space.

Mary got near Tammy and kneeled to her knees and said, "We'll help you get through this."

Leslie stroked Tammy's hair.  "We'll be downstairs when you're ready to talk." Tammy shook her head in agreement and the ladies went back to the kitchen where the guys were.

In the kitchen, Brian and Mark were on the bar stools at the kitchen counter.  Brian was digging into his food from IHOP.  There were two cigars rolled up on the counter next to Brian's cell phone.  Mary noticed Tammy's purse while walking over to start the microwave to reheat the food.  She warmed up the pancakes and the omelet.  She then took Tammy's purse and the food up to the room that Tammy was in.

Mary knocked on the door.

"Come in."

Tammy was texting fast like a teenager with a new cell phone. Mary walked into the room to hand Tammy the container of food. She then turned around and placed the purse on the dark wood dresser.

"Thanks girl! I forgot all about my purse and the food." She finished typing and put the phone on the bed next to the food.

"His ass has 48 hours to call me!"

"You're giving him an ultimatum?"

"Yes! His ass is ignoring me."

"Um...you kinda pushed him into doing whatever he's doing."

Someone knocked on the door.

"Come in," Tammy said.

Leslie came back upstairs.

"I'm full." Leslie looked at Tammy and said, "You didn't touch your food."

"Nah, but I will," answered Tammy.

"So, what did he do Tammy?"

"He was at a strip club blowing money."

"That's it!  You can get past that."

"Plus, he moved a lot of money out of our joint account.  I don't know what he plans on doing with that money, but he took enough to put a down payment on a house.  Maybe he wants to start a new life with another woman."

"Damn, what are you gonna do?"  Mary asked.

"Divorce him!  If he doesn't call me back within the next 24 to 48 hours, I'll file for a legal separation, then a divorce.  That gives him 48 hours."  The look on her face was as serious as cancer.

Leslie said, "Let me tell you something."  She walked over and sat on the edge of the bed near Tammy.

"I've always admired your relationship with Steve.  You two have been together since high school.  You told me about some of your arguments, but that's what married people go through, right?  You two were able to work through those issues, right?  You two have been together for over 20 years.  That shit is special!  No kids to raise, no real drama, and to add to that, y'all got plenty of money! Y'all should be trying to have another baby, not planning a divorce."

Mary said, "I know after your son drowned, things were rough between you and Steve. You two made it through that...remember? Besides, do you know how hard it is to find a man out here? It all starts out good, but we all have some skeletons in our closet at our age. You don't know what these guys have tried behind closed doors. You got a good man, Tammy. That's some she-say he-say gossip that Jas heard."

Leslie jumped back in the conversation.

"The point we're trying to make is, you don't want to throw in the towel and start all over again because you went out with a man and Steve went to the strip club. Now the money that is missing from your account, that's some different shit. If he blew all that money on strippers and hanging out, that would definitely be an issue. But you need to find out the real deal, you know...the truth, not some salon gossip. You're like a sister to me and I wouldn't steer you in the wrong direction."

Mary got up and said, "On that note, I'm going downstairs to enjoy myself."

Mary did a funny dance on the way to the door. That put a smile on Tammy's face. After that, Mary walked out of the room. Tammy opened the container and took a few bites of the omelet and pancakes.

Leslie was staring at Tammy. She was trying to figure out what type of mood Tammy was in. Tammy took a few more bites and got off the bed and so did Leslie.

Tammy said, "Alright, I came out here to have a good time and to forget about my issues. Let's go downstairs!"

"That's what I'm talkin' about!" Leslie was getting excited. Tammy walked out of the room with her food in one hand and her phone in the other. Leslie followed.

Now, they were all on the second floor of the beach house. They were all sitting or standing in the kitchen once again.

Mark spoke up and said, "Lets spark one. It's cool to smoke inside?"

"Yeah, it's cool. I don't mind," Tammy said to Mark and Brian.

"By the way, thanks for the food!" Tammy replied. She smiled with a nonchalant demeanor. Tammy walked to the microwave to reheat her food.

Mark said, "You look like someone killed your vibe."

Tammy said, "If you keep making comments like that, all fingers will be pointing at you. Let's talk about something else."

Mark was surprised by the comment, "Ouch! You're definitely feisty."

Tammy changed the subject. "Where are y'all from, down south?"

"Yeah. Texas, over there by the Cowboys' stadium," Brian replied. He lit the cigar.

"Yeah, I knew it. Y'all do sound a little country. Go Cowboys!" Tammy played along as she took control of the conversation and started asking them questions.

"What are y'all doing way out here by the beach?"

Brian passed the weed and stretched. "We're friends with Sean Jakes."

"Who's that?" Tammy questioned.

Mary looked unsure too. She said to Brian, "I think he was the one throwing the party...right?" Mary looked at Brian and Mark for confirmation.

Ding! The microwave was done warming the food. Tammy took her food out of the microwave. Mark stood up and gave more details while putting his stuff in the trash.

"Yeah, we all grew up together on the same street. We go way back. Sean was a barber back in the day, and his brother was a coach in the NBA. So, his brother gave him some money to open his own shop. My boy opened three barber shops and two salons. Then he started getting info about vacation rentals, and he bought a few. That's how he got that beach house where the party was. He decided to throw a party before renovating that joint." Mark sat back down when Mary passed the weed to him.

Tammy started eating more of her food. "It's good to hear the brother is doing well." Tammy looked at Mark and smiled. She cut the pancakes and put a fork full in her mouth.

Leslie looked at Brian. "How do you fit into the picture?"

Mary walked over to the Samsung smart TV, turned it on, and logged into the Netflix app to hear some stand-up comedy.

Brian focused on Leslie "Like he said, we're from the same neighborhood."

Leslie got more specific with her question, "What do you do for a living?"

He replied, "I own a car wash." Brian looked at Mark, "Well, we own a car wash."

Mary chose to watch the "Queens of Comedy." When she pressed play, all eyes went to the TV.

Mary said, "These ladies did their thing! This one right here is a classic!"

They all agreed. Mary joined the conversation again.

"Y'all a long way from home."

Brian gave her his attention. "Yeah, we flew out here to kick it with Sean."

"Oh, that's a fancy rental car y'all driving," Tammy implied.

Mark said, "Nah, I left the car here when I drove out here last month...had a family emergency. Had to cut the trip short and fly home."

Leslie interjected, "Where y'all get the weed from? Let me guess...Sean?"

Mark was getting frustrated. "Yeah, Colombo! We're out here having fun with our homie, and I came to drive the car back home. Who is the one with all the questions now?"

Mark was shaking his head while looking at Leslie and Tammy.

Brian jumped into the conversation. "I know right! Y'all some damn good looking cops. You can put the cuffs on me now, but be gentle, officer of the law."

Brian stretched out his wrist toward Leslie and they all started to laugh.

One of the female comedians told a funny joke which made them all laugh again. They all focused on the TV for a while, which made the mood a little more enjoyable. Everybody finished eating except Tammy. Mark reached into his pocket for a lighter to light the weed he had rolled up. He took two long pulls and passed it to Leslie.

Tammy finished her food and put the container in the trash. She went to the refrigerator to grab a bottle of water.

Mary yelled out "Can you pass me one of those too?"

Mary gathered her trash from where she was sitting and took it to the trash can. She noticed the guys dumping the ashes in one of the plastic food containers because there were no ash trays in the beach house.

"Here, dump the ashes in here." She passed the container to Leslie, and she did just that.

Tammy checked her cell phone. Leslie passed the weed filled cigar to Mary.

Tammy excluded herself from the group again and walked out onto the balcony. The guys and Mary migrated closer to the TV. Tammy was out on the balcony looking at the stars. She swiped the screen on her phone. No missed calls and no text messages.

Tammy decided to text Calvin.

"Are you up? I need your help. My marriage might be over."

She paused and looked around at the view of the nice luxury beach houses and the ocean that was in the far distance. She could hear the water crashing against the rocks. Leslie stepped out onto the balcony where Tammy was.

"I came to check on you. Do you want to smoke?"

Leslie took a pull. Tammy did not utter a word. She just reached her hand out and grabbed the rolled up weed with her index finger and her thumb.

Leslie asked, "What are you out here thinking about?"

Tammy took one short pull, held the smoke in, and passed it back to Leslie. Leslie did the same. They held the smoke in their lungs for at least 5 seconds. Laughter came from inside the beach house.

The female comedians kept the mood festive. Tammy blew the smoke out first. Then Leslie did the same thing.

"I now know what it feels like to have money and not be happy."

Leslie looked at Tammy with sorrow.

"You're my sista and a sista's love can help you get through anything."

Tammy moved back from the rail of the balcony and took a seat in one of the brown wicker chairs with soft red cushions that were positioned perfectly on the balcony.

"Thanks, girl!"

Tammy looked at Leslie with sincere remorse.

"I made a mistake and now he won't talk to me or return my texts."

Leslie sat down and grabbed her hand. "He'll come around. Give me his number. I know a guy who's a cop. He could probably do that triangulation stuff to find his location, you know, that CSI stuff."

They laughed at what she said.

"Remember what we were talking about earlier? When you get him back, you better give him some great sex.  Make him feel like a king."

Tammy had a big grin on her face.  "I got you girl!"

Tammy stood up and stretched like she had a long day.  "I'm going up to the room."

Leslie got up and followed Tammy into the beach house.  Leslie passed the weed to Mary which interrupted the conversion that Mary was having with the guys.

Tammy walked toward Mary and the guys.  She stood in front of the television and smiled at all of them.

"Thanks again for the food.  I'm going to bed.  The sun will be up soon.  Y'all have fun.  Don't do anything that I wouldn't do!"

They all grinned.  Everybody said goodnight. Tammy dismissed herself and slowly walked up the stairs.  She got to her room, closed the door, then proceeded to take her clothes off. After tossing her clothes on the floor near her medium sized luggage, she locked the bedroom door and turned on the shower.

After that, she checked her phone to see if Calvin or Steve had contacted her.  No new text messages were found. She stood in the shower surrounded by steam and hot water before going to bed.

Mary and Leslie wanted to have a little fun of their own. They turned off the TV and went into different bedrooms to keep the party going. After two hours went by, the sun started to make its appearance along the horizon. Mark stepped out of the room looking satisfied, but Mary was clearly disappointed. The look was written all over her face. Mark walked down the hallway, pulled out his cell phone, and called Brian to see if he was ready to roll out. Mark stopped in the kitchen area. Mary walked to the front door of the beach house as if she was ready for him to leave.

Brian answered the phone, "Yeah, I'll be downstairs in a minute."

He had to put his clothes on in a hurry after realizing that sex was not on the menu for him and Leslie. Leslie went to pick up the shirt she took off while they were playing strip blackjack. She put the shirt on and walked to the bedroom door.

She placed the deck of cards on the dresser and held the door open for Brian. As he walked by, she patted him on the shoulder and said, "Better luck next time, playa."

Brian looked at her with a slight grin and said, "Whatever! So, what's your number so I can get a rematch."

Leslie smiled back and said, "Nah, we're good Brian. I had fun, but you're not my type."

Brian was shocked. "What! I see you like to play games. You're a big tease!"

Leslie dismissed him quickly. "Well, have a safe trip back to Texas."

"You're really not gonna give me your number?" Brian asked a second time.

"Brian don't beg. It's pitiful."

Brian looked at her and shook his head side to side.

He was disgusted when he said, "I sure did waste my time with you."

She toyed with his emotion. "Now, don't be bitter because you lost. You gotta step your game up."

"Yeah, alright. I'm out!"

Brian tried to walk downstairs to meet Mark in a cool and calm manner.

"Man, let's roll!"

Mary opened the door. Brian walked past Mary and said, "Alright pretty girl!"

Mary gave him a head nod. Mark was the last to leave. He leaned in and tried to kiss Mary. Mary turned her head and allowed him to kiss her cheek.

Mary looked at Brian and Mark. "Be safe out there in those streets!"

Mark stood by the door and said, "Hit me up!"

Mary shook her head in agreement and then closed the door in his face.

Leslie came downstairs. The smile on her face was devilish. "I heard some commotion over there in your room."

Mary frowned her face up. "Yeah, he was a minute man. He was hitting it right, but he came first and then he couldn't get it hard again. So, I made him lick my pussy, but he fell asleep. I told his ass to get up. I'll take a shower to finish the job myself."

Leslie was laughing. "I know what you mean. You nasty girl!"

Mary said, "Girl...bye!" Mary locked the front door and headed back to the room to take a shower.

Leslie shouted out, "I'll see you in a few hours!" Leslie walked to her room smiling and laughing. She was glad that she did not waste her goodies on Brian.

Later on that morning, the ladies awoke with a story to tell. They gathered in Tammy's room to talk about what happened when Tammy went to bed. After a few good laughs in Tammy's room, it was time to get the day started. The phone rang. Tammy was hoping it was Steve or perhaps Calvin. It was Kim. She suddenly thought about Kim and the things she was going through. Her emotions and thoughts switched. Tammy was more concerned about Kim and her situation.

"Hey! Girl, I'm glad you called! I told myself that I was going to check on you today." Tammy mentioned. Tammy put Kim on speaker phone so they could all hear and talk to her.

"Hey girl! How you doing?" Leslie said.

173

"And I'm here too!" Mary shouted.

Kim said, "Hey, y'all must be having a good ol' slumber party like we used to do in college. I remember those days."

Tammy said, "Yeah, I guess you can say that, but it is not the same without you."

Mary said, "Did you hear any good news about your sister?"

"No, Morgan is still missing, but we have a lead that we're going to follow. So, I'm just giving updates to let people know what's going on. We're leaving in the morning to meet the detective."

Leslie said, "Okay, we'll send a prayer up for ya!"

"Thanks, y'all know I need all the support I can get!"

Tammy said, "Whatever you need, just let me know okay!"

"Thanks Tammy. Hey, I'm gonna get moving. I'll be in touch."

They all said goodbye to Kim and ended the call.

## CHAPTER 7

## KIM

At the crack of dawn, Kim was up and at it. She was moving with a purpose. Her and Lawrence brought a change of clothes and put everything in one suitcase.

"How do you feel babe?"

"I feel nervous and anxious all at the same time. I don't know what to expect. I just want to meet Frank and get some answers."

"Are you hungry?"

"I don't want breakfast food right now. I had a protein bar and two cups of tea with a lot of sugar. I have the jitters right now."

"I know how this situation might make you feel uncomfortable. Despite what happens, I'll be here for you Kim. Come on, let's make this trip."

They got into her BMW and Lawrence took the wheel. Kim looked at the address for the funeral home that was written on a sheet of paper. She then typed the address in into the GPS to guide them on their way. They were headed down 95 South around 8:00 am on a Sunday morning. Kim called Frank to tell him that they were on their way.

"Hello," he said in a raspy tone.

"Sorry to wake you, but we should be down there around 11 am."

"That's fine. I'll see you when you get down here. Let me get up and get myself together."

"Okay. I'll see you soon."

"Okay Kim. Bye."

Kim and Lawrence had a few short conversations during the ride to the funeral home, but Kim's mind was somewhere else. One hour went by as the sound of smooth jazz filled the air while they drove in silence.

The silence between them was not uncomfortable, but rather a shared understanding that words were unnecessary at that point in time.

When they made it down to the funeral home, Kim and Lawrence sat in the car for a moment to gather their thoughts. The mood was quiet. Kim knew that she would never forget the sensation of those goosebumps on her skin due to the overpowering chill that had momentarily consumed her.

It was a reminder of the reality and the mysteries that lie just beyond her comprehension.

Lawrence looked over, "You okay babe?"

"Yeah, I just got cold that quick. I pray that today..."

Kim stopped mid-sentence and grabbed his hand. She closed her eyes, bowed her head, then began to pray.

"Lord, you know we come to you in prayer to seek closure for the disappearance of my sister. Please let today be the day that we get our questions answered and we find Morgan. In Jesus name. Amen."

They both took a deep breath and exited the car. There was an overcast that day. It made the surrounding area look gloomy. Lawrence walked around the property and found the front entrance to the building. He walked around to the other side of the building and found another entrance.

Kim stood by the car staring at the funeral home. She let Lawrence take control of the situation by letting him brief her on what he saw and what they should do next.

"Kim, what's up? What do you want to do? There are some cars over there on the other side of the building near the entrance. I saw the hearse over there too. We can go up to the front or knock on the door over here."

Lawrence pointed at a door that was close to where they parked.

"Where is Frank? Did he say he was on his way?"

Lawrence was giving her options and asking questions, but Kim was not the independent business woman that she normally is. At that particular moment, she was acting like a scared little girl.

Lawrence saw what was going on, so he walked over and grabbed her hand, then started walking to the door. They took a few steps, then Lawrence stopped walking to talk to Kim.

"You got that lady's number...right? Give her a call and tell her we're here. Call Frank too."

Kim nodded, "You're right. Let me call Mabel and Frank."

She looked up at him when she was finished dialing Mabel's number and said, "I'm afraid. You should know that I'm preparing myself for the worst."

Lawrence shook his head in agreement.

"Hello."

"Hi Mabel, it's Kim from the hospital. How are you?"

"Oh, Hi darling! How are things going?"

Well, we're outside the funeral home. I was wondering if you could meet us outside where the parking lot is.

"Honey, I'm not there. I'm at home. We live twenty-five minutes away. Look around and tell me if you see a pretty gray Cadillac?"

Kim looked around the parking lot and noticed two cars. A red Honda Accord and an old blue Ford F150.

"No, I see a red car and a blue truck, but no Cadillac."

"Okay hold on.  I thought my husband was there," Mabel said.

She got out of bed and grabbed her robe. She put the robe on, grabbed her phone, and walked to the front door.  The Cadillac was in the driveway.  She saw her husband outside talking to one of their neighbors.

"Oh, child.  He's still here.  I'm looking at him right now.  He's talking to our neighbor from across the street.  Give us some time and we can meet you down there."

"Okay."

"In the meantime, if you walk to the side of the building, there's another door.  You said you saw a blue truck.  That means William is there.  He's been working with us for years.  He'll let you in.  The other car belongs to the new guy.  I don't remember his name, but just knock on the door and ask for William."

"Okay, hold on.  We're walking over there now."

Lawrence and Kim walked over to the door.
When they got to the door, she tried to turn
the knob, but the door was locked.  Kim
knocked on the metal door.  No answer.
Lawrence gave it a shot and knocked with more
force.  He knocked the way the police knock
on doors when they announce themselves.
Still no answer.

Kim put the phone to her ear and said, "The
door is locked.  We knocked, but nobody
answered the door.  I know there is someone
in there because I can hear music playing."

"Yeah, they play music sometimes when they
are handling the bodies over there.  I'll
call there to get them to open the door.
I'll call you back."

"Okay."  Kim replied.

Kim scrolled through her recent calls and
called Frank.

"Hello."

"Frank, it's Kim."

"Hey Kim.  I'm at the diner not too far from
the funeral home.  Where are you?"

"I'm at the funeral home now waiting for someone to let us in."

"Oh, you made it down here already. You were not playing when you said you'd be here in the morning. Let me finish up here and I'll be over there in a jiffy. Did you eat this morning? The food is good at this diner. I've been coming here for breakfast every morning since I've been out here."

"I'm not hungry right now. I just want to find out what happened to my sister."

"I understand. I'll be there shortly."

Lawrence and Kim looked at each other. Lawrence said, "Let's wait in the car."

Kim agreed. They started to walk back to the car. After taking about nine steps, the sound of a metal door opening stopped them in their tracks.

They turned around and there stood a black man that was at least six feet tall wearing blue jeans and a black long sleeve shirt. He came outside and started stretching. The door slammed shut. He looked in their direction, pulled out a cigarette and said, "Y'all friends of Mabel?"

Kim answered, "Yeah!"

"Come on in, I'll show you around till they get here." He shouted back.

Lawrence and Kim walked toward the man standing near the metal door.

"Are you Kim?"

"Yes."

The guy put the unlit cigarette in his mouth, wiped his hands on his jeans, and extended his hand to shake Kim's hand. After shaking hands, he took the cigarette out of his mouth.

"I'm William. Mabel called and said to let y'all have a look around. She said they're on their way. Do you mind if I smoke one real quick?"

"Nah, go ahead," Lawrence replied.

William opened the door and shook Lawrence's hand as they walked inside. William pulled out a lighter to light his cigarette as he let the door slam shut. The sound of the metal door closing startled Kim. Once they got inside, Kim stood there in silence while she looked at everything that was in the

183

large creepy room. Lawrence walked around
observing all that he could see. There was a
desk and two big metal chambers toward the
end of the room that were used for cremation.
The area resembled a science lab with white
walls. There were instruments, gloves, long
rods and all sorts of metal contraptions that
were placed neatly all around that area of
the funeral home. There was a brown casket
on a gurney close to where Kim stood.
Lawrence walked off to the left to look at
some items on the self. That is when Kim
noticed another guy in the room walking
around with a box on the right side of the
metal chamber. He walked into another room
that was far from where she was standing.
Kim walked to the right where the guy was.
Along the way, she saw boxes that were big
enough for a human body. She walked closer
to where the guy was, then she heard the
metal door open, and slam shut again. She
turned around and noticed that William was
standing next to Frank.

Frank was an average size Hispanic detective
with gray and black hair wearing blue jeans,
a red dress shirt, and sunglasses. His gold
rope chain was shining along with his badge
that was clipped to his belt.

She walked to where the guys were standing.
Lawrence was introducing himself and shaking

Frank's hand by the time she got to where they were standing. Kim gave Frank a long warm hug.

"Hey Kim! Well, let's get this show on the road," Frank uttered.

They started walking further into the room. Then William asked,

"What's this all about?"

Frank was holding a manila envelope in his left hand.

"I'm glad you asked," replied Frank.

Frank walked over to a desk that was close to the door. He opened the manila envelope and made all the contents slide out onto the desk. There were a few pages of the police reports and pictures of Daymon, Gene, and Morgan.

Frank said to William, "The last time we were here with the county police, you were not here."

"You're right, so what are you saying?" William retorted.

"William, we have reason to believe that these people were here a few weeks ago."

Frank picked up three pictures and held them with both of his hands.

"Do you recognize these people?"

He then used his right hand to put the picture of Gene close to William's face.

While holding the other two pictures in his left hand.

"Have you seen this person?"

"No." William answered.

Frank swapped the picture of Gene and showed a picture of Daymon.

"How about this person?"

"Nah. I've never seen him."

Frank swapped the pictures again and showed a picture of Morgan.

"Now, how about this person?"

William started to squint to get a good look at the beautiful picture of Morgan.

"Nope, never seen her either. Who is she? She looks like a model."

Kim spoke up, "She's my sister and they brought her down here and did something with her body and her car! This was a waste of time!" Kim was getting mad at this point because the guy was not helpful at all.

Just then Mabel and her husband walked into the room wearing matching black and white tracksuits.

Kim was greeted with a motherly hug from Mabel. "What's wrong child? You look mad."

"Still...no answers!" Kim shouted. Lawrence started to console Kim.

The husband was pointing at Frank. "I remember you. So, you're back again with a smaller entourage."

Frank nodded his head and said with a serious tone, "Yes sir!"

Robert gave his attention to Kim who was being hugged by her lover.

"Hello Kim. Mabel told me what happened."

He reached his hand out to shake her hand.
Kim let go of Lawrence's hand to shake his
hand.

"I'm Robert. We're willing to help in anyway
possible. I don't think my guys would be
involved with my nephew Eugene, but feel free
to look around and ask questions." Robert
was a black senior citizen with gray hair, a
gray beard, and a gray mustache with a belly
that protruded over his waistline.

Kim replied, "Nice to meet you."

Robert said, "Well not under these
circumstances, but the pleasure is all mine.
Now, how can I help you all?"

"Think about it. Gene came down here around
the same time my sister disappeared.
Coincidence! I think not!"

"I agree, but he wasn't here long," Robert
mentioned.

The other guy came out of the room after
hearing all the commotion. Frank saw him and
asked Robert, "Who is that?"

He was an average sized white guy, in his early forties, wearing a blue colored lab coat with a pair of blue jeans. His dirty blond hair was down to his shoulders. He was standing with a metal box of ashes from a body that was cremated earlier that day.

"That's Stan." Robert shouted, "Stan, come join us over here for a second!"

Stan proceeded to walk toward them. He noticed six people gathered around the desk in the lower level of the funeral home, near the crematory. Stan took a quick look at all of their faces. He did a double take when he glanced at Kim. His eyes widened and he almost dropped the box.

Robert said, "Put the box in the back where it belongs and come back to talk to the detective."

Frank still had the pictures in his hand. When Stan came back, Frank handed the pictures to Stan as soon as he was within arm's reach.

Frank asked, "Have you seen these people around here?"

Stan looked down at the pictures and quickly said no without lifting his head.

Frank gave Stan a stern look. "Are you sure?"

Stan gave the pictures back and looked only at Frank.

"Yes, sir."

Stan nodded his head, turned around, and walked back to the room where he came from. He was walking with his head down. Everyone noticed that his body language was off. Kim followed him.

"Please...if you know something, let us know."

It was obvious that he was ignoring her as he walked away. Kim caught up with him. Then she put her hand on his shoulder to turn him around.

"I know you know something."

Stan turned around with a blank look on his face. They both stared at each other for a few seconds. He looked down and reached into the pocket of his lab coat to get a label. After that, his eyes focused on the shelf that was behind her. He walked past her, grabbed a box from the shelf, and put the label on it. He took a deep breath, then turned around to face Kim again.

"I'm sorry, but I can't help you."

Kim rolled her eyes as she looked around the room. She realized that she recognized the room somehow, but she couldn't remember how she had this room in her memory. Then it came to her. It was like Deja Vu. She was in a similar room in her dream that she had in the past. It was revealed right in front of her, but this time, it was not a dream.

Kim was in a daze for a moment. When she came back to reality, she looked at him and said, "I'm sorry, can you repeat what you said."

He said, "Look, I don't want to get in trouble."

He looked at Kim with tears in his eyes as he continued to speak.

"My house is in foreclosure and my wife has a bunch of medical bills. Those guys came here, and the gay guy said that his uncle and aunt run this place. I've seen him here before, and he had keys to the facility. He said he needed me to get rid of the body.

Robert and Mabel were not around. The other guy gave me fifty grand in cash. I couldn't reject that. The girl was already dead. He gave me an offer that I couldn't refuse. I cremated the body while they stood and watched. I had a feeling this was wrong, but they gave me the money that I needed to get out of my situation. I'm sorry!" He dropped to his knees.

"You look just like her. Please forgive me."

He wrapped his arms around Kim's legs. Kim shook him loose and kicked him to the floor.

By that time, everyone else made their way to the small room to see what was going on. Frank stepped in first.

"What's going on?" Frank asked.

Kim said, "He cremated my sister! This mother fucker helped them get rid of her body!" She kicked him in the stomach.

"Is that right?" Frank asked.

The guy cried out while he was still on his knees. "Please forgive me! I needed the money. She was dead when they brought her here. I didn't kill her!"

Kim kicked him in the stomach again.  Frank did not bother to stop her.  He stared at Stan and replied, "But you helped them dispose the body which is a felony offense punishable by up to five years in prison, my friend."

Robert pushed past Frank and Kim and grabbed Stan by his shirt and pulled him up onto his feet.

"Why didn't you say something?  What the hell where you thinking, Stan, doing that type of stuff in my establishment?"

"How could you do something like that?  You know how to reach us if we're not around!" Mabel yelled out.

Stan repeatedly said he was sorry, while Robert was clinching Stan's shirt.

Frank stepped out to use the phone to call the local authorities.

"Stop honey!"  Mabel pulled Robert off of Stan.

Robert was furious.  He released the grip he had on Stan's shirt.

Stan fell to the floor and curled up in the fetal position as he continued to cry. He knew he made a terrible mistake.

Robert looked down at Stan and said, "You're going to lose your freedom because of this Stan. I thought you were smarter than that."

The grimaced look on Robert's face was evident. He looked at Mable, Lawrence, and Kim.

"Now it makes sense! Daymon and Gene got a tour of the funeral home because they were talking about starting a business like this in their area. They both asked a considerable amount of questions about the cremation process. Despite the unforeseen circumstances, I answered all of their questions as accurately as I could. I was not aware of the situation. I showed the guys the crematory and told them it takes about two hours to burn the corpse. I explained that some families like to watch or initiate the cremation process. I didn't think they would use my place of business to dispose of a body. My phone rang that day while I was talking to them. I answered it and excused myself from the conversation. I gave Daymon one of my business cards that was on the desk as I walked up the stairs.  I was trying to get a better signal on my cell phone."

Lawrence walked closer to Kim.  She immediately fell into his arms.  She was weak in the knees.  Lawrence had to hold her up to keep her from falling to the floor.

## CHAPTER 8

### DAYMON

Daymon woke up from his comma five days after the ordeal at the funeral home. He didn't know why he was in the hospital. Every time he closed his eyes, he saw a glimpse of what transpired days ago. He didn't remember much, but images of different events were replaying in his mind. The nurse came into his room to check his vitals. The doctor and another nurse that was on the floor joined in to make sure he was stable. One of the nurses left the room once things were under control. She called one of the police officers that had been frequently coming to Daymon's room while he was in a comma. The police had been waiting to arrest him for kidnapping and desecration of a body. Not too long after that, the police officer notified Frank and told him about Daymon's condition.

Frank was at home cooking on the grill when he received the news that Daymon was awake and stable. Frank said to the officer on the phone, "Good, I'll be up there as soon as I can." Frank didn't call to tell Kim the news immediately, knowing that she was already distraught after the situation at the funeral home.

The hours passed by. Night had fallen over the city and Daymon was moaning throughout the night. Daymon was suffering from seizures, double vision, and headaches. After the doctor reviewed some X-rays, he told the nurse, "The neurological and cranial nerve examination showed signs of paralysis. Daymon's brain is swollen and that's why he's having those issues with muscle spasms and seizures. I don't expect him to recover from this. I sure hope he can make it through the night."

On that day, Daymon was in and out of consciousness most of the time. Later that night, he was stable and was able to sleep. While he was sleeping, Daymon was having flashbacks from the day when Morgan came to his house unannounced and caught him by surprise.

# CHAPTER 9

## MORGAN

During his flashbacks, Daymon remembered Morgan calling him that day when she showed up unannounced. She left a voicemail telling him that she would be there in two hours.

"Hey D, I decided to come up a day early. So, I'm on the way...can't wait to see you. Call me when you get this message. I'm in Delaware, so I should be there in about two hours."

The day was warm which made for a nice ride. Morgan's cell phone beeped to indicate the battery was low and the phone will shut down soon. She realized that she forgot to bring her car charger. So, she put the phone on the passenger seat, turned up the music, and put the pedal to the metal.

Two hours later, Morgan pulled into the driveway at Daymon's house. Morgan saw someone's SUV in the driveway. She curiously looked in the SUV and noticed a Rihanna CD in the passenger seat. She was confused. None of her, nor his friends owned a Range Rover. She got closer to the front door of Daymon's house and heard music playing.

Morgan turned the door handle. Surprisingly, the door was unlocked, so she quietly walked in. As she walked through the foyer, she noticed the bathroom door on the main level of the house was open with the light on.

Morgan crept to the living room. She called her sister, but the reception was bad. Kim could not understand what she was saying.

Kim said, "Hello...hello."

Morgan said, "I'm at Daymon's house. There's someone in the bathroom. I can hear them peeing."

Morgan didn't hear her sister reply. Then the call ended because her phone died. The door was open wide enough for Morgan to see a man dressed like a woman standing in front of the mirror fixing his wig.

Morgan was confused, thinking why is there a brown skin medium built guy in the bathroom dressed like a female?

Kim called her right back but the phone when straight to voice mail. Kim left a message.

"Hey girl, I think you called me by mistake. I couldn't hear what you were saying. Call me back if you need something."

Kim remembered her sister's phone reception is always poor whenever she is at her boyfriend's house. At that time, Kim didn't think it was a big deal.

Morgan had a nervous gut feeling while she slowly walked through the house. She went into her purse to grab her mace. Morgan walked to the staircase and yelled Daymon's name. The guy came out of the bathroom and crept up behind her and stood at the bottom of the staircase and said, "Oh, he didn't tell you about me?"

She turned around and stared at the guy and said, "Don't come any closer! Where's Daymon?"

"Daymon is upstairs going both ways boo!"

Just then, Daymon came out of the master bedroom and stood at the top of the staircase. The homosexual mistress walked toward Morgan. She sprayed him with a large amount of mace which sent him screaming to his knees. Morgan ran to the top of the stairs and started arguing with Daymon as she

stormed past him.  She went to the master
bedroom and grabbed her two purses and threw
her clothes into the Goyard travel bag that
was next to the dresser.  Daymon was trying
to get her to stop what she was doing and pay
attention to what he was saying.  She tried
to spray him with mace, but Daymon dodged the
mist.  Morgan swiftly moved around Daymon,
but he grabbed her arm and headed downstairs.

She snatched her arm from his grip, then ran
to the closet where he kept his gun.  She put
her hand on the top shelf, but she did not
find the gun.

Daymon was yelling at the top of his lungs.
He was trying to get her to stop and listen
to him.  She turned around in the hallway and
gave him the evil eye as he explained that he
had been bisexual for a while and did not
want to tell anyone.  He wanted to avoid the
embarrassment and judgment from his friends,
his family, and his colleagues.

Morgan replied by yelling, "What about me?
You were not going to tell me shit!  Now I
have to worry about getting AIDS because of
your trifling ass!"

"I use condoms," he said.  She rolled her
eyes with disgust.

Morgan said, "I can't believe this shit!"

She walked toward the stairs and Daymon grabbed her arms again with force.  Morgan was facing him, not knowing what was going to happen next.

"Let me go...you faggot!"

Those were the words that came out when she got loose from Daymon's grasp.

Suddenly, the other guy made his way up the stairs and yanked the back of Morgan's hair when she wasn't looking, causing her to tumble backwards down the stairs.  When Morgan got to the bottom of the stairs, she was not moving.  Daymon ran down the stairs to get to the bottom quickly.  He checked her pulse.  He put his ear near her mouth and nose to see if she was breathing.

"She's not breathing!  No!  No!  I think she's dead!"  Daymon tried CPR to revive her, but no response.

"Why did you do that!  Look at what you did!"

"You need to choose Daymon!  You can't have your cake and eat it too!"

"Fuck all that Eugene!  She's dead!"

They stood in silence staring at the lifeless
body that was at the bottom of the stairs.
They were waiting for her to breathe or move.

"I can't deal with this Daymon.  You deal
with this shit!  I'm leaving!"

"Like hell you are!  We're both going to
prison if we don't handle this right.  Your
ass ain't going nowhere until we figure this
out!"

# CHAPTER 10

## GENE

It was nighttime in New Jersey. Gene and Daymon were plotting. Gene said, "We need to make this look like a murder, as if someone broke in and committed this brutal crime."

"Nah...Gene, we need to make this disappear." The room was silent as they stared at the body with disbelief.

"Why the fuck did you do that?" Daymon asked.

Gene said, "There's no time to blame each other. You tried to live the best of both worlds, and this is what happened."

Daymon fell to his knees crying like a grown man would if his wife had died. As he slowly moved closer to Morgan, he reached out his arms to bring her body closer to him. While he looked at her body from head to toe, he said in a low tone, "Why did you come here today?" He was rocking back and forth on his knees looking like a nervous wreck.

Gene shouts, "You know what, I know someone with a cremation unit."

Daymon was confused. "What the hell are you trying to do?"

"Listen, my uncle has a funeral home. I remember them cremating bodies when I was younger. You know what? We can take the body down there and burn it. It would be like she just disappeared."

"Where do we have to go?" Daymon asked.

Gene sighed, "Way down in Virginia."

They pulled themselves together, got some bed sheets to wrap up her body, and moved her car into the garage so no one would be able to see what they were doing. They spent all night cleaning the house and preparing to make that trip with a dead body in the trunk.

During the discussion with Gene, Daymon said, "We need to figure out what we're going to do with her car once we cremate her body. Gene, we need to take two cars. You need to follow me down there and we can cremate her body, clean her car, remove the tags, then burn it. We can't leave any fingerprints nor DNA behind."

Daymon continued to take control of the
situation. "Get two of the those Go Phones.
We can throw them away if we need to. If we
do it this way, we won't have a phone record.
A prepaid phone is the way to go to make this
happen without a trace. So, before we burn
her body, we need to stop using our cell
phones. Don't tell anyone about this. Hell,
don't even use your phone anymore. Turn it
off and use the Go Phone! Alright!"

"You're not going to blame all this on me
Daymon...right!" Gene said in a sarcastic
way.

"I ought to push your ass down the stairs for
doing this shit! Get the phones! Act normal
and keep your mouth shut or your ass will end
up in jail in a matter of time."

Gene gave Daymon the puppy dog, I'm sorry,
look and walked out of the house. The glow
from the street lights caught his eyes as
the kids started to migrate to their
respective homes. He looked around, sighed,
then walked to his vehicle replaying the
event in his head. It was hard to comprehend
how things had gone so horribly wrong so
fast. Gene got into his Range Rover and sat
there for a few minutes. He pulled his phone
out and called his aunt Mabel to ask for a
favor. Gene told his aunt that he had a

friend who was interested in the funeral business. He had set up an arrangement with his aunt to have Daymon meet with his uncle Robert to talk about running a funeral home.

They let a day go by before they made the trip to Petersburg, Virginia. It was a rainy Monday morning. Daymon and Gene got a tour of the funeral home. They both asked questions about the cremation process. The sound of a cell phone ringing broke the monotony of the conversation. The uncle answered his phone and promptly told the caller to hold on for a second.

"Daymon, here is my card. If you have the desire to get involved in this type of business, this is how you can reach me." He excused himself from the conversation as he walked up the stairs to get some privacy.

Daymon told Gene in a low secretive tone, "We have to do it tonight or tomorrow. We have to get back to New Jersey and act like nothing happened."

"Yeah, easier said than done," said Gene. "We're going to sneak around here and burn this bitch up into dust and you expect us to go back home and act like nothing happened...like we didn't kill her and do some premeditated shit!"

Daymon raised his voice, "It's your fault we're in this shit!  You killed her Gene!"

Gene quickly put his index finger to his mouth and made a gesture for Daymon to be quiet, like a mother would do to a kid in church.

Daymon lowered his voice.  "You're the reason why we're down here in the country at a funeral home with Morgan dead, wrapped up in bed sheets, in the trunk of a car."

After the argument, the guys went outside to the car where Morgan's body was.  They stood outside looking around the facility.  After scoping out the area, they figured out how they were going to bring her body into the funeral home.

Daymon scanned the area like a hawk and pointed to one side of the building.  "There aren't any cameras on this side of the funeral home."

Gene said, "We're out in the country.  It's safe.  Everyone doesn't have a top flight security systems out here."

Daymon stood and looked around.  The rain had stopped, and clouds gave way to a little sunshine.  There were a lot of trees surrounding the parking lot that would aid them in being inconspicuous with their plans to dispose Morgan's body.  They walked around to the front of the property.  Robert was saying goodbye to someone that came to the funeral home as he yelled out to Gene, "I'm going inside to make some calls.  I reckon' you boys aren't going to hang around here all day.  It was nice to meet you Daymon!"

"Same here, sir!"  Daymon replied.

Gene had an idea.  "Hey, you still have that gift card for Olive Garden?"

Daymon frowned.  "Yeah...why?"  He went into his wallet as Gene explained.

"My aunt and uncle love to eat at Olive Garden."

Daymon gave the gift card to Gene.

Gene said, "I need to persuade them to take this card and go out tonight.  We'll have all night and half of the morning to get it done.  My uncle will show up between seven and ten in the morning."

Daymon told Gene to make it happen as he patted him on the ass like a football player does when his teammate does something good on the field.

Gene went back inside the building. Daymon stood in silence looking at the trunk of Morgan's car. His body got cold, and he began to feel nauseous. The thought of what transpired over the last 72 hours broke him down. He walked closer to the car and leaned against it. He closed his eyes and tried to shake off the ill feelings.

He began to visualize the look on Morgan's face when she fell down the stairs after Gene yanked her hair. He got off the car, took three steps toward the trunk of Morgan's car, then suddenly threw up.

He fell to his knees, wiped the vomit from his lips and said, "Forgive me father for my sins. Have mercy on my soul."

While in the hospital, Daymon had more flashbacks of when he and Gene got rid of the body, torched the car, and headed back to New Jersey. A few days later, the police detained Daymon and grilled him with a bunch of questions. Daymon cooperated with the police. He had an alibi. His neighbor said he saw Daymon's car in the driveway and saw the lights on in the house. He also said later that night, he saw the lights were out.

Little did the police know, Daymon was controlling the lights from his phone.  He had definitely crossed his T's and dotted his I's.

# CHAPTER 11

## FRANK

It was a Sunday afternoon. The weather was warm, and the sun was shining. Kim, Lawrence, Tammy, Leslie, and Mary were back in Maryland. While waiting for Kim's arrival, Frank was at the hospital getting the info from the other detectives that were working the case. They could not get a real statement from Daymon because he was not able to talk. Daymon answered a series of questions by blinking twice for yes and three times for no. Kim made it to the hospital with Lawrence. They met up with Frank outside of the hospital. He gave Kim a warm fatherly hug and he shook Lawrence's hand.

Frank looked into their eyes and said, "So, he admitted to killing Morgan. He's in bad shape. I don't think he's gonna make it out of this hospital."

Frank escorted them to Daymon's room. The hospital hallway was well lit with decent abstract paintings on the wall with chairs that were spaced far apart from each other. They walked and talked about the funeral arrangements. They also talked about some

of the events that took place at the funeral
home.  They got to the floor and checked in
at the nurse's desk.  Frank led the way.  Kim
and Lawrence followed.

Once inside the room, Kim walked closer to
Daymon.  His eyes got bigger as he noticed
the resemblance between Kim and Morgan.
Frank and Lawrence stood alongside the wall
that was near the bathroom, which was about
six steps from the hospital bed.

Lawrence turned on the lights when he noticed
how dark it was in Daymon's room.  The noise
from the machines that were keeping him alive
could be heard from all angles of the room.

She stood over him.  His eyes were opened and
focused on Kim.

She yelled, "How could you?"

She wanted to choke the life out of him.
Instead, she spat in his face like Mabel did.
Then she smacked his face with the back part
of her hand.  Daymon turned his head to face
Kim again after she smacked him.  Tears
started to stream down his cheeks as he
started to whimper.

"Don't start crying now you bastard! You
don't get to cry!" Kim cocked her hand and
back slapped him again.

Frank stepped between Kim and Daymon so she
could not hit him a third time. She was
outraged and was ready to fight. Lawrence
wrapped his arms around her from behind like
he was giving her a bear hug.

He gently moved her away from the hospital
bed because he heard one of the nurses coming
to see what was going on.

The nurse saw her patient crying and trying
to form a sentence, but he was having a hard
time getting the words out. Frank approached
the nurse and assured her that the situation
was under control. Frank watched Lawrence to
see if he was able to get Kim to calm down.
The nurse looked at Daymon's face and saw
that his face was red. Daymon was trying
desperately to move around in the
uncomfortable hospital bed. They all saw him
come to tears because he could not move his
arms, legs, nor torso. Frank closed the
hospital room door and spoke in the nurse's
ear. He told her what Daymon did. She stood
up straight and looked at Frank in shock,
then turned her head to look at Kim.

She said in a professional tone of voice, "Ma'am, I'm sorry for your loss.  But, I can't allow you to beat a paralyzed man on my floor while I'm on duty!"

Kim shook her head in agreement and then Lawrence took his arms from around her.

"I'm Sorrrryy!"  Daymon was able to get the word sorry out, but it was slow and slurred.

They all looked at him to see if he was going to say something else.

Unfortunately, that was all that he managed to say.  He was breathing heavily like he was straining and trying with all his might to get the words out.  The beeping noise from the heart monitor was getting faster.  Kim took a few steps to stand at the foot of the hospital bed to watch him suffer.

"You're getting what you deserve.  I hope you go to hell!"

The nurse started to check his vitals.  She then said, "I'm going to have to ask you all to leave the room."

Frank opened the door and said, "Come on y'all."

Lawrence grabbed Kim's purse as all three of them walked out of the hospital room. By the time they got into the elevator on that floor, they heard the announcement.

"Code Blue!  Code Blue!"

Code Blue was heard several times from the hospital's wide response system. A response team was rushing to Daymon's room. The elevator door closed, and Kim started smiling as she pressed the button for the lobby.

"Are you alright?"  Frank asked.

"Yeah, I am now. I hope his ass dies in that room with his pitiful looking self," Kim replied.

"I've never seen you act like that. I saw evil in your eyes, babe. I definitely don't want to get on your bad side any time soon," Lawrence added.

They got to the lobby of the hospital. Hugs and handshakes were exchanged. Kim smiled with some relief.

"Thanks for everything, Frank!"

Frank smiled back.

"No problem.  I told your dad I would look after you...and I always keep my word!"

"Yeah, he would be proud.  I'm lucky he had a friend like you."

Frank said, "I'll keep you posted with any forthcoming information."

Lawrence looked in Frank's eyes and said, "Thanks for helping us get closure with this situation."

"I told you...no problem.  Just stay in touch and take care of Kim.  That's all I ask for."

"Okay!  Bye Frank."

Kim and Lawrence separated from Frank and walked to their vehicle.

# CHAPTER 12

## TAMMY

Tammy was at home, on the couch, watching a movie drinking a glass of wine while she waited for her sister to come over to touch up her hair.  She was bare foot wearing black sweatpants and a black sports bra with multiple colors.

Steve did not call, and she was lonely and mad at herself for not thinking about the consequences of her actions.  The phone rang and she almost dropped the glass of wine while rushing to get the phone off the ottoman.  She was hoping it was Steve, but it was a call from Calvin.  She got moist between her legs just thinking about what could happen between the two of them, since her husband was not in the picture anymore.

"Hello stranger.  I'm glad you called."

"Tammy this ain't Calvin, this is his sister Pam.  Remember me from the cookout?  Anyway, my brother got robbed and he got beat up pretty bad.  I'm going through his phone to see who was the last person that he talked to.  I called people to find out what they know, but no one knows anything."

"Oh my GOD!  When did this happen?"  Tammy asked.

"Two or three days ago.  Let me get to my point.  I started reading his text messages. I found a text with multiple pictures of you. I thought about it, then I raised an eyebrow. I thought you were married?"

Tammy replied, "I am, but we're not speaking to each other.  I think we're done."

There was silence on the phone.

"Oh...okay.  I see.  You and my brother have been messing around.  He never told me about you and him."  Pam kept digging for information, "Where's your husband?"

Tammy was shocked that Pam asked that question.  She put the glass down on the table next to the couch and sat on the edge of her seat.

"I don't know.  We haven't been talking to each other.  If I find out anything about Calvin, I'll let you know."

"Please do.  Word to the wise, keep your married ass at home and stop whatever you and my brother are doing.  Nothing good can come from this."

Pam hung up the phone. Tammy sat motionless trying to grasp what she had just heard. She wondered if Steve played a part in that incident. She doubted that he would go that far with this situation. She got up and started pacing around the house. She said to herself, Steve wouldn't rob anyone. He doesn't need the money.

She realized her sexual desire for another man didn't turn out good for her because she is in the house alone with no man to call her own. She got on her knees and said a prayer.

"Lord, I know I haven't been to church in a while, but I'm asking for forgiveness. I messed up my marriage. I'm praying for my husband to forgive me and come back home. Amen."

She decided to call Steve one more time. This time he answered the phone from his car.

"What? Why do you keep calling and texting me?" He said in a harsh tone.

"I'm sorry, Steve! Please come home so we can work this out!"

"What about your boyfriend? You think I'm gonna let you fuck another man and I'm gonna just come crawling back because you said you were sorry? I don't need you, nor the drama you bring. This money got you thinking that you can do whatever you want, huh?"

There was silence on the phone.

"I don't think I want to come back. I need more time to think about it." He ended the call.

Tammy went to get the bottle of wine and drank straight from the bottle until it was empty.

Steve was on his way to a cigar lounge that afternoon as he was driving away from Omega's neighborhood.

The clothes that he and Omega wore the night they beat up Calvin were in a trash bag in the trunk of his black Maserati. When Steve ended the call with Tammy, he remembered that he needed to get rid of the trash bag. He drove to a random apartment complex that day and tossed the clothes in a dumpster. Steve pulled out one of his cigars, cut it, lit it, then sat on the hood of the car to think about what he was going through.

He felt mad and confused. He was unsure of the future with his wife. He decided to stay on the move. Staying busy was the only way for him to block the negative thoughts in his mind. The cigar calmed him down and gave him the buzz that he wanted. Going to the cigar lounge was not part of his plan anymore.

The day was young, and the cigar was getting smaller in length. Since he did not have an ash tray to let the cigar smolder, he decided to put the cigar out by crushing it on the asphalt pavement. Shopping was on his mind. Steve was sitting in the Maserati when he received a call from Omega. Steve answered the phone in the car.

"Yo."

"A boy, what ya doing?"

"Just throwing out the trash...you know."

"Oh yeah. Good thinking!"

"I was going to a cigar lounge, but now I feel like shopping. You down for that?"

"Hell yeah! Let me jump in the shower."

"No doubt. I'm coming back to pick you up."

"Alright, let me get myself together."

"Yeah, do that."

They ended the call and ended up at the mall before it was dark. Steve gave Omega $1000 and paid for all the new shoes and outfits. He knew his cousin would keep his mouth shut. In other words, it was money well spent.

They met some females that day at the mall while they were shopping. Later that day, Steve got a call from one of the females. Their conversation lasted for hours that day and the following day. As a result of their chemistry, they decided to meet again.

Omega had other plans that day, so Steve had to ride solo for the first time in a week.

They decided to meet at a well-known sports bar called High Score for appetizers and drinks. Steve got there first. He sat at the bar wearing blue jeans, a light yellow dress shirt and brown Gucci loafers; no wedding ring. The bartender came by, wiped down the surface where Steve sat, and gave him a menu.

"What are you having today sir?"

Steve picked up the menu and started
squinting.

"Ah, let me look at this menu.  By the way,
I'm waiting for someone.  So, I'll take a
margarita and the nachos for now."

"With salt or without sir?"

"Go ahead and add the salt."

"Will do.  I'll get started on that order."

The bartender walked away.  Steve continued
to look at the menu with anticipation of
good food and good company.  He got
distracted when the people in the restaurant
started cheering for one of the local teams
that was playing on the flat screen
televisions in the restaurant.

She made it to the restaurant fashionably
late with an outfit that made a statement.
Her name was Sherri.  She was a slim, light
skin female with permed hair that went passed
her shoulders.  She was wearing high hill
shoes that displayed her manicured toes and a
tight blue denim jumpsuit that was sexy and
classy.  All eyes were on her as she walked
to the bar.  The bartender came back with
Steve's margarita.  He placed it on the bar
with a small napkin and stood like a statue

staring at Sherri as she walked closer to Steve.

Steve slightly swiveled the bar stool to see what he was staring at. When Steve noticed it was Sherri, she gave him a seductive grin which made him stand up to greet her. They hugged and looked at each other from head to toe.

Sherri and Steve were checking each other out and giving each other compliments.

"You got every man in here checking you out."

"Well, you should feel lucky because I'm spending my time with you and not one of them."

"Oh, you're real fancy huh."

"Nah, I'm just looking cute for our date. That's all."

"You're being modest, I get it!"

It was clear they were attracted to each other. They took a seat at the bar, then the bartender pulled out another menu and placed it on the surface of the bar.

"Hello ma'am!  I'll give you a few minutes to look at the menu."

She glanced at the menu and chose what she wanted to eat.  Steve did the same.

She said, "I think I'm gonna go with the Cobb salad and the salmon."

"That's a good choice.  I'm gonna pick the fish tacos."

She smiled.  "I was gonna pick that too.  I see we do have some things in common."

Steve smiled and nodded his head in agreement.

He gazed in her eyes and sighed.  "I want to be straight up with you.  I'm married. Things aren't going well with my marriage. I'm embarrassed to say this, but my wife is fucking her personal trainer.  She left and went on a trip with her girls.  I haven't been home in a while.  The marriage is practically over.  When I saw you at the mall, I had to say something.  I wanted to see you again and again."  After he explained his situation, she did the same.

"Well, I'm recently divorced and I'm not trying to get involved with a married man."

She sucked her teeth. Sherri looked disappointed. She stood up as if she was ready to go.

"Thanks for being honest. Most men would just keep lying or won't bring it up at all. You must be one of the special ones."

"I'm just being real with you. I just found out about my wife's affair. It fucked me up to the core."

Sherri could tell that he was devastated by the whole ordeal. She walked closer to him, then she put her hand on his shoulder to wish him good luck. Steve put his hand on the side of her waist. He looked in her eyes and gently guided her to the seat that was close to him. Sherri noticed his tenacity, and the scent of his cologne was enticing.

The waiter came back with the appetizer.

"Here are the nachos sir. Wow, you're gorgeous ma'am. Would you like to start with a drink or an appetizer too?"

"Thanks for the complement! I'll have the Cobb salad and the Salmon with broccoli as my entree. Oh, and I'll take a Lemon Drop Martini too."

"What about you sir?"

"I'll have the fish tacos."

"Very well.  Let me put this order in for you two."

Steve gazed passionately at Sherri.

"Sherri, I don't want a rebound chick.  I just want someone to be with.  You can feel the attraction...right?"

"Yeah, I do."

"Let's just eat this food and talk.  You can put a chair between us, so it doesn't look like we're here on a date.  It'll look like two strangers sitting here eating some food at the bar.  Come on, just sit and talk to me.  It's my treat!  You can get the steak and lobster.  It's all on me."

She laughed and decided to stick around.  She did what he said.

She sat one chair down from him.  They were trading stories and conversing like two friends from high school.  She enjoyed his company, which made him more attractive to her.  After eating an early dinner and three drinks later, they decided to end the evening. Steve got the bartender's attention by waving his hand.

"Can I get the check?"

Steve pulled out two one hundred dollar bills and placed the money on the bar as the bartender printed the receipt.

"You know what, the drinks were good! You can keep the change!"

Steve gave the waiter a big tip for the great service. Sherri was impressed, to say the least. She thought the date was appealing to her, despite Steve's situation.

They got up from where they were seated. Sherri was wearing a pair of Manolo heels which accentuated her body. She lost her balance for a second when she stood up, which caused her to grab the chair as she started to laugh.

"Whoa, I'm a little tipsy."

Steve grabbed her hand, "I ain't gonna let you fall. Come on, I'll walk you to your car."

Steve asked, "Where did you park?"

Sherri pointed to the left as they were walking out of the restaurant holding hands. She stopped walking and let his hand go to make sure she had her keys and phone with her.

"All right, I parked over there too."

Steve was checking out every curve her body had to offer while she looked in her small Fendi purse that was strapped across her body. Sherri pulled out her lip gloss and made her lips shine.

She said, "Follow me!"

Sherri led the way, and Steve kept the conversion going while being hypnotized by the way Sherri's ass was moving in the denim jumpsuit. It was evident that she was wearing a thong or no panties at all.

They made it to her car. Steve opened the door of a white Mercedes and said, "I hope we can stay in touch."

Sherri gave him another seductive smile and stared at him for a few seconds. She hesitated. "Sure! You got my number. What about your wife?"

"Like I said, she can have her personal trainer, and I can have you."

"Oh, I'm the rebound chick, huh?"

"No, more like a new beginning."

Sherri liked what he was saying and felt that he was sincere. She sat in the car, started the engine, and looked at Steve eye to eye.

"It's all the same Steve. Listen, I've never done this before, but there is something about you that turns me on."

Steve smiled at her. "Yeah, I'm attracted to you too. That settles it. I'll call you later."

Sherri smiled and closed the door. Steve walked away real cool with swagger. A car drove by Steve and stopped. Then, the driver put the car in reverse. It was Lawrence and Kim. Kim was driving her BMW. Sherri was pulling out of her parking spot and heading to her next destination.

"Hey Steve! What are you doing out here?" Kim asked.

Steve looked around to see if Sherri had left. "I came out here to meet a friend.

I know I parked my car around here somewhere."

He played it off until he knew the coast was clear. He pulled out his key FOB and set off the alarm for his car.

"See, I was close. The car is over there in the next parking aisle."

Steve got closer to the car to talk to them. Lawrence was on the passenger side. He moved his head closer to the driver's side window to speak to Steve.

"Yeah man, I know what you mean. It's a huge parking lot. It's easy to forget where you parked out here if you're not paying attention. I haven't seen you in a while. It's good to see you!"

Steve replied, "Likewise!" Steve looked at Kim, "Did they ever find Morgan?"

Steve watched her demeanor change. Kim looked disappointed when she answered his question. It was clear that she didn't really want to talk about it.

"No, but we found out that her boyfriend killed her." Kim changed the subject. "So, we're going to have a vigil soon.  We would love to have you and Tammy there."

"We aren't on the best of terms right now. I'm pretty sure your girl told you what's going on."

"To tell you the truth, Tammy is depressed, and she isn't herself without you.  Go see her Steve!"

Steve looked up at the sky and looked back at Kim.  He shrugged his shoulders.  "Maybe next week.  I don't know.  Let's see which way the wind blows."

"I'm too through with you Steve...bye!"

She drove into the same parking spot that Sherri parked in.  Steve started to walk away.  When Kim and Lawrence got out of the car, Steve turned around and yelled out, "Enjoy the food!"

Kim just threw her hand in the air and waved.

Lawrence yelled, "No doubt!  Alright man. See ya!"

Kim and Lawrence walked to the sports bar and Steve jumped in the driver seat of his Maserati.

## CHAPTER 13

## THE CALM AFTER THE STORM

It was a warm sunny Saturday morning, two weeks after Kim and Frank uncovered the disappearance of Morgan. There was a large crowd of people that showed up at the church that Kim and Morgan were members of. There were not enough seats for everyone because there were so many people there to celebrate the life of Morgan. People had to stand up along the walls or sit in the aisle on one of those uncomfortable folding chairs. Tammy was sitting up front in the church pew with Kim and her family. Mary, Leslie, and some other females associated with both Morgan and Leslie, all sat in the same row together. The majority of the females were wearing something white or an entire white outfit. There were white and silver balloons that adorned every corner of the church. Large pictures of Morgan were up front, in the center, surrounded by candles and more white balloons for all eyes to see. During the vigil, the preacher gave some comforting words and a few people spoke about the good times they shared with Morgan. The service came to an end. A woman opened the double doors near the front of the sanctuary. Two women stood in the lobby with a large amount of white balloons. The preacher instructed everyone to stand up and walk to the front of the church, where the pictures were, to get a balloon. Steve was in attendance that day. He got in line and stood along the wall with the rest of the crowd near the front of the church. After Kim noticed him, she grabbed two balloons from the ladies and walked toward Tammy. When she got near Tammy, Kim grabbed her hand and continued to walk. Tammy was frowning. She was not sure where Kim was taking her, but she followed her anyway.

Tammy asked in a low tone, "Where we going?"

Kim did not answer. With two balloons in one hand and her best friend's hand in another, Kim gracefully escorted Tammy down the line to where Steve was standing. When Tammy realized what Kim was doing, she stopped dead in her tracks. She was shocked to see him. Tammy was vulnerable during that moment with feelings of sorrow. She felt like a little girl who did not know what to do.

Kim faced Tammy, "Come on girl, talk to him."

Kim gave a gentle tug as she continued walking and greeting people until they got close to Steve. He was wearing a blue suit, white dress shirt, with a brown belt and brown shoes.

Kim gave the two balloons to Steve. Then she gave him a hug and thanked him for coming to the vigil.

She turned to Tammy and said, "I love you like a sister."

She made Tammy and Steve join hands. Not knowing what to say, Tammy stood silent with tears in her eyes. Steve noticed how beautiful she was with the small red purse on her shoulder, red heels, and a white dress that fit her body perfectly. He gently pulled her closer to him and gave her one of the balloons. Kim walked back to the front of the church thanking people along the way.

Leslie, Mary, Jasmine, Tammy's parents and brother watched to see what was going to happen. Tammy hugged Steve and sighed. Steve kissed her cheek and hugged her tighter. The preacher approached Kim and asked if she would like to say a word or two. Kim stood at the podium with a smile on her face.

"Amen!"

Kim said when she saw Steve and Tammy hugging like two people in love.

With the microphone close to her lips, Kim said, "It's an honor to see so many faces in

this church today.  I know Morgan left some
type of happy memory of her in your mind.
I'm pretty sure she would want that to be the
last memory of her.  She has moved on to be
with the Lord.  As we bring closure to this
vigil, I want you all to follow me outside
and think about the last time you saw Morgan
smile or any good memory you have of her.
Once you've got the memory locked in, I want
you to let your balloon go and hopefully that
memory will stay with you for a very long
time.  Just like these balloons floating in
the air for a considerable length of time."

Everyone did just that.  They went outside
and released over 100 balloons to signify
that Morgan's soul was free, but the memories
of her will live on.

Kim, Lawrence, Tammy, and Steve went on a
vacation to the Grand Cayman Islands that
following year.  All expenses were paid by
Steve as a token of thanks for bringing him
and Tammy back together.

They had made plans to have dinner together
on the first night.  Tammy and Steve were
eating appetizers patiently waiting for Kim
and Lawrence.  The Spanish style villa was
situated near the water with a pool, outdoor
kitchen, and more.  The weather was
cooperating.  The palm trees and the ocean in
the far background created the perfect

scenery for this occasion as the sun was starting to set.

"Hey, it's about time y'all showed up. I thought you two were gonna lock yourselves in the room and get it on until the break of dawn."

Kim and Lawrence laughed while they continued to walk toward the table that was set up in the back of the villa. The outdoor kitchen was perfect for alfresco dining. The ocean view complemented the heated pool and jacuzzi that was illuminated by a purple neon light, which was a few steps away from where they were sitting.

"That would be nice, to tell you the truth!" Lawernce said with a devilish grin. Kim softly punched Lawrence's arm.

Kim was embarrassed. "Why are you feeding into that?"

"I'm just playing babe."

Steve laughed. "You two can do whatever you want. We're grown right?"

Lawrence smiled. "You said it!"

Kim and Tammy continued to laugh. Lawrence pulled out Kim's chair and held her hand as she sat down.

Lawrence walked closer to Steve to give him a manly hug. The private chef and his assistant came over to the table in their chef attire to tell them what they had planned to cook for them.

"What an amazing view you have here. Do you agree?" The chef asked with a Caribbean accent.

"Yes, I'm glad we came out here!" Steve replied.

They all spoke to the chef and listened to him as he explained what they were going to make for them.

"You guys are going to be pleased! Tonight's menu will be extraordinary! We'll be preparing conch stew, red snapper, jerk chicken, conch salad, and mixed vegetables."

The assistant chimed in with her thick Caribbean accent, "Oh, we can't forget the rice and peas! Do you want some freshly made rum punch?"

Steve nodded his head and said, "Yes. Thank you. That would be nice!"

After the chef's assistant nodded her head, the chef walked off to man the grill while the assistant took care of everything else inside the kitchen.  Lawrence gave Steve a pound from across the table.

"Thanks for inviting us, Steve.  This villa we're staying in is top-notch!"

Kim was checking out their surroundings.  She focused on Steve and Tammy and started smiling.

"Y'all know this place is spacious.  You guys are on one side of the villa and we're on the other side.  We really can't hear you unless you laugh or raise your voice.  We really needed a vacation, and this is the perfect place to be...the Cayman Islands!"

Steve had a big smile on his face.

"Well, I just wanted to show my gratitude for helping us get back together."

Kim looked directly at Tammy.  "It means a lot to have real friends who'll stick with you through the toughest times.  I'm truly thankful that you two are the type of friends that I'm talking about.  Thanks for checking on me when we were trying to find my sister."

Tammy replied, "It seemed like we were both going through a storm at the same time. Me and my marriage...you and your sister."

Tammy stood up and walked over to Kim. Kim stood up and they hugged like two sisters that haven't seen each other in years. Kim backed up a little to rub on Tammy's baby bump.

"This is my last vacation before the baby comes."

The chef's assistant came back with the drinks. She came out with two fancy pitchers. One with rum punch and the other pitcher had cucumber lemon water. The chef came back to the table after he put the food on the grill. He poured a glass of water and the assistant poured rum punch in the other 3 glasses. The chef gave the water to Tammy and everyone else grabbed the rum punch and stood up to toast with the chef. The chef had one more glass for himself. He filled the glass halfway with the cucumber lemon water. He raised his glass and said, "May the saddest day of your future be no worse than the happiest day of your past!"

They all nodded their heads in agreement and said, "Cheers!"

The chef drank the water and then walked back
to the grill.  The assistant also went back
to work in the kitchen.  Kim and Tammy sat
down while the guys started a different
conversation.

Kim said, "That water looks good girl!  I
know you're in your second trimester.  Do you
know the gender of your baby?"

"Actually, we do!  I was waiting for this
moment.  I wanted to tell you in person.
We're having a girl, and we're going to name
her...Morgan."

www.ingramcontent.com/pod-product-compliance
Lightning Source LLC
Chambersburg PA
CBHW020756250626
47155CB00003B/1097